monsoonbooks

THE MAN WHO COLLECT

Nigel Barley was born south of London in 1947. After taking a degree in modern languages at Cambridge, he gained a doctorate in anthropology at Oxford. Barley originally trained as an anthropologist and worked in West Africa, spending time with the Dowayo people of North Cameroon. He survived to move to the Ethnography Department of the British Museum and it was in this connection that he first travelled to Southeast Asia. After forays into Thailand, Malaysia, Singapore, Japan and Burma, Barley settled on Indonesia as his principal research interest and has worked on both the history and contemporary culture of that area. After escaping from the museum, he is now a writer and broadcaster and divides his time between London and Indonesia.

PRAISE FOR THE MAN WHO COLLECTED WOMEN
'Writing today about such a historical figure as Alexander Hare – and indeed about a fictional European male in late-colonial Asia such as Arthur Grimsby – can be a fraught undertaking. Barley is clearly aware of this, and diffuses much of the potential tension with a certain satirical playfulness. Hare is eventually undone by the agency of Anna and Maria, recent South African additions to his harem, while Arthur is bested by just about everyone. And the book's unexpected finale is a sharp lesson never to make unthinking assumptions about apparently passive background figures.' Tim Hannigan, *Asian Review of Books*

ALSO BY NIGEL BARLEY

The Innocent Anthropologist
A Plague of Caterpillars
Not a Hazardous Sport
Foreheads of the Dead
The Coast
Smashing Pots
Dancing on the Grave
The Golden Sword
White Rajah
In the Footsteps of Stamford Raffles *
Rogue Raider *
Island of Demons *
The Devil's Garden *
Toraja *
Snow Over Surabaya *

(* published by Monsoon Books)

THE MAN WHO COLLECTED WOMEN

NIGEL BARLEY

monsoon

monsoonbooks

First published in 2020
by Monsoon Books Ltd
www.monsoonbooks.co.uk

No.1 The Lodge, Burrough Court,
Burrough on the Hill, Leicestershire LE14 2QS, UK

ISBN (paperback): 9781912049745
ISBN (ebook): 9781912049752

Cover design by Cover Kitchen.

A Cataloguing-in-Publication data record is available from the British
Library.

MIX
Paper from
responsible sources
FSC
www.fsc.org   FSC® C018072

Printed and bound in Great Britain by Clays Ltd, Elcograf S.p.A.
22 21 20   1 2 3

To Jamie James:
'Friendship is far more tragic than love.
It lasts longer.'
Oscar Wilde

Introduction

Alexander Hare (1775-1834) was a real person though it is unclear how much of him remains real and he is treated here with novelistic freedom. Born a watchmaker's son in London and of Scottish heritage, he and his brothers established a trading house that extended as far as India and what we now know as Indonesia, at that time the Dutch East Indies. Alexander rose to prominence during the brief period (1811-16) when the British, in the form of the East India Company, ruled Java under the governorship of Thomas Stamford Raffles who would go on to become famous as the founder of Singapore. Hare has long been an enigma to historians since so little hard evidence about him remains and he became demonised by the Dutch as a convenient stick with which to beat the Raffles administration, so that both individuals and governments had self-seeking motives to spread sensationalised rumours about him. Most centre on his love of women and his assembling of a harem, after the oriental fashion, that he sought to establish on an uninhabited atoll in the Indian Ocean and so create his own personal paradise. This has made him an object of guilty male fantasies and of strident female resentments, the epitome of masculine, colonial exploitation. Yet we live in a world today where all generalization is rape and perhaps the picture we have of him should be more complex and contextualised and the boundaries of our categories more open to question and more historically nuanced. Hare's dream became a nightmare as most dreams do, though not without its own enduring legacy. It led to the populating of the Cocos-Keeling Islands, now part of Australia, where – in an example of the porosity of boundaries – the descendants of that first enterprise are now campaigning for reclassification as a recognised, indigenous people. A central element of the traditional culture that supports their claim is Scottish country dancing.

Chapter One

Arthur Grimsby had always imagined there would come a point in his life where he would suddenly feel grown-up. He would know who he was, what the world was all about, would suddenly see how everything made sense and had purpose and he would probably feel driven to communicate this wisdom to the grateful young. This was the first evening of his fifty-fifth year, sitting in far Singapore, contemplating a whole new decade – the 1960s – and that magical moment had still not come despite the experience of love, war, imprisonment, marriage and death. A new decade always tried to be portentous but was often merely an intimidating blank page.

So how had he spent the day? Wallowing in the fulsome congratulations of others? The indulgence of the senses in fine food, drink and sexual gratification? The purchase of some long-desired but overpriced object? No. Birthdays could be a time of taking stock and finding that the cupboard was bare. So he had gone to the office as usual, where his birthday had not been acknowledged in the slightest way, and had worked on his manuscript dealing with the life of an obscure 19th-century British trader in the Eastern seas, one Alexander Hare. He had returned home to a mantelpiece uncluttered by cards of saccharine birthday greeting. Not that he minded. He was not a social creature. And how would he spend the evening? Making up for the neglected opportunities of the day in riot and mayhem? No. He would simply carry on with his work at home. He knew now that that magical moment of divine enlightenment would never come and he began to wonder whether the acceptance of that knowledge was all that being fully grown-up really meant.

There came a click from downstairs, the manservant, old Bok Ong, switching on the outside lights, creeping round the house like a dry stick insect at the end of the day. He had come with the house, almost as part of the furniture, staying on, quite untroubled, when it was requisitioned by a Japanese officer during the war and sometimes, when polishing the floors, he would hum an odd little Japanese tune acquired during that interregnum and clearly regarded himself as the real owner or true child of the house. Bok had scrubbed and rubbed that floor so long it was as if he had rubbed himself into it, until it became a thing of wonder in the city, a black teak mirror pitted, not by the usual coarse nails but by countersunk brass screws and he tended it day and night. Visitors to the house cooed over it but Bok did not encourage visitors, especially white ones, as they trampled over his floor with their shoes on. It had taken time but he had trained *tuan* better than that.

The house itself was an ancient Singapore pile, Tudor black-and-white on high pillars whose plaster had a surface of fluffed potatoes, a building in shorts, its bare legs keeping the inside cool and saving it from the sudden monsoon floods. A generous verandah ran around three sides beckoning in air and light with monsoon blinds to keep out the rain. It was absurdly big just for one man and his servant but still too small for the books that had overflowed onto chairs and down onto the floors. Books did not harm the rich patina of the floor and so were permitted. Soon Bok Ong would come and adjust the slatted shutters, nodding, 'Good evening, *tuan*', swatting and tutting loudly, to keep out the enthusiastic bugs. And then there would be dinner.

The two of them ate different food, each in ridiculous, solitary splendour at different ends of the house, one in the dining room, the other in the kitchen, using different tools and switching plates for bowls. First, Arthur would eat, having sloughed off his jacket and then Bok Ong, having thrown off all but vest and underpants as unnecessary affectation. Since the death of his wife, Arthur dined sparingly on the tinned meat and potatoes of the *mems'* dining room via Cold Storage. It was not worth making a meal of one man staying fed. Nowadays, food irritated him as a distraction from work. Bok Ong meanwhile would feast voraciously on proper Asian dishes, sinking its roots down into every culture that had ever swept over this little island and gathering up every creature that flew or scuttled into its maw.

Yes, it was foolish but both knew that eating together was impossible – apart from being a social short-circuit – because it would create the need for conversation and they barely had a language in common and now Bok was growing deaf so that everything was said in triplicate. Arthur, anyway, was stolidly monoglot, except for a smattering of schoolboy French that retained the Manchester accent he had ditched in his pronunciation of English, with a little market Malay. People nowadays were incorrigible verbivores, made a big hoo-hah about the need for chit-chat, but none was necessary in Arthur's household as each knew exactly what to expect from the other and, anyway, Arthur liked to continue thinking about his work at home. Perhaps that's the way it had been in the polyglot household of Alexander Hare.

His wife, Eileen, had grown irked by the old man creeping silently about the house like a hungry ghost and had wanted to fire him, hire someone young and energetic who would whir and click to her orders instead of blandly ignoring them.

'All he does is wax that sodding floor over and over again and you should see the look he gives me if I come out of the bathroom with wet feet and tread on the bloody thing – my own floor!'

Arthur was shocked by the suggestion and they had fought over it, every other ground for contention being contested under cover of the issue. He suggested compromise. Arthur was no slave-driver and had tried to hire other staff to take the burden off Bok Ong's thin back – aged Chinese retainers somehow had the ability to be thinner than any starving man inside Changi jail under the Japanese – and offer him rudimentary society but the old man had set his face against it. The Indian washerwoman had been driven away by the slamming of doors and hard looks. The harmless, sweet-natured, Malay gardener was forced to eat his tiffin sitting under the house, drinking water from the garden hose.

Bok Ong had worked here now for over thirty years and had his own iron routine and each day he started at the same point and followed in the same track like a slow, clockwork toy until he reached his bed again at nine and slipped into it in a way that disturbed the sheets as little as possible and rewound himself during the night with ratcheting snores. Arthur wondered. Could anyone so restricted and solitary be counted a free man? Young people equated freedom with change and sociability but experience suggested to Arthur that freedom came from acceptance, from making one's dreams small, as he had learned to do in Changi jail and preserving an inner space for oneself, as he had learned to do in marriage.

Perhaps Bok Ong was the one who was really grown-up. His only known recreation was to occasionally wander by the harbour when out shopping, where he ate an ice cream sandwiched between two slices of Indian bread, skilfully rotating it to catch the drips, while collecting the names of ships from foreign parts he would never visit, writing them down with sticky fingers in a little notebook with the great solemnity of a little boy collecting train numbers.

Bok entered the room in his white jacket and adjusted the lights, switching off the central fitment and turning on the glowworms of the table lamps, making it impossible for Arthur to read where he sat.

'Good evening, *tuan*.' He slid a plate bearing a sausage roll on to the table. 'Dinner one hour.'

***

Arthur found freedom and slavery in 19th-century Southeast Asia a puzzling issue as he chewed on Cumberland pork. It seemed that just who was and who wasn't a slave was a slippery question but one that could be carved up to advantage like most slippery questions, for doubt always meant opportunity. Of course, the children of slaves were also slaves but what of those misbegotten on slaves by freemen? That slaves might beget on free women was culturally defined as biologically impossible but there were credible rumours about certain of the Batavian widows – all pious yafraus by day but allegedly slaves themselves to forbidden passion under the blanket of night. Those enslaved by local law were clearly slaves – prisoners of war, debtors, women and children sold into slavery by husbands to pay their own gambling debts or feckless men who enslaved themselves in hard times to avoid the responsibility of caring for their own lives – but what of those kidnapped, simply carried off and sold? Perhaps they were not slaves until they had passed sufficiently far down the chain to accept their own status as such. But there was no doubt that the object of his study, Alexander Hare, had been a slave-owner.

As a trader in the early years of the century, he probably realised that the crucial point of maximum profit was that of transition from free to slave. Still, there were complexities. Anyone could own Asian slaves, including fellow Asians, but even the Dutch – freshly defeated by the British – could not actually *be* slaves themselves for there were acknowledged racial limitations and designated hunting zones – Nias, Bali and the mountain Toraja. You could not expect to just go hunting for slaves in Central Java because that was already on the map. But in Borneo? Of course. In Borneo, the upriver peoples were wide open to trapping as being part of Nature, truly orangutangs, merely wild creatures of the forest and therefore fair game.

Arthur tried to think himself into Alexander Hare's head as he, a 19th-century man, ran his jaundiced eye down the line of beings on offer as gifts from his host, Sultan Soleiman of Banjarmasin, and carefully appraised thigh and breast. The idea of slave ownership would probably have excited him in a way he had not felt since he assumed command of his first vessel with full rights in bottom and he felt his chest expand like a billowing foresail. Arthur coaxed forth a similar guilty excitement in his own chest. This was surely another rite of passage at the time, part of truly becoming a man, an awakening. But now the smile disappeared from Hare's lips and a petulant storm settled on his manly brow. He did not have to examine teeth and feel limbs as the buyers did in the Batavia slave market to see that these were not product of the first chop, not freshly hunted but a ragtag mob swept up from the leavings of the sultan's own subjects and would have cost His Bornean Majesty precisely nothing. Though inexperienced in such matters, Hare was – for God's sake – a grown man in his forties and had been stripping females in his mind's eye all his life, peeling aside stouter clothing than this. He recalled, as a boy on his way to school, watching a man in Smithfield meat market auctioning off his wife amongst the ripped and steaming cattle carcasses and piles of slithering guts, he having last-minute doubts, she tearing open her blouse, parading all she had up and down and declaring roundly she would suffer him no longer and wanted change. She had fetched five shillings and a yard of ale and seemed pleased at the result and delighted that she even got some of the ale. Hare had been terrified to move, fearing they might take his slightest twitch for a bid – with all the terrible responsibility that would bring.

Some of the men looked roughly serviceable enough for farm labour, but the women lay at the far end of their appealing usefulness, all of them sullen and more a burden than an asset. They might be from a sultan but their wrinkled faces made you think more of sultanas. Some would be divorcees or widows, reduced to this by the lack of alternative in their marital misfortune. Some looked so embittered they might have been born divorcees. Any man who took them into his household would be clasping a nest of angry, hissing vipers to his bosom. He was obviously being used as a pension scheme for the sultan's own convenience.

Hare sucked his teeth and shook his head. A quiver of outrage ran through his stomach. As one of the Resident Commissioners of King George's Britannic Majesty in the Eastern Seas, Alexander Hare, had clout and was anyway known here as a merchant with a sharp eye for margins, trading in pepper, spice, wood, anything from beeswax to birds' nests that would yield a profit as God intended for Man to do. Moreover, the sultan was beholden to him for his stock of the East India Company's main local product, opium, a source of both profit and pleasure for the entire royal household. He would not be taken for a fool and stamped his foot and felt another rip tide of anger surge within him. But this was the Indies and, here, a man who lost his temper lost respect. Hare checked himself, smiled sweetly, tossed back the thick, wavy locks that were his crowning glory and addressed the smirking chamberlain in courtly Malay – all honorific avoidance of the bruising active mood and surrounded by charming floskel and curlicues – and with a deferential inclination of the head.

'Pray tell His Majesty as follows. First, that I am touched by his offer of this magnificent gift of slaves who, I see clearly, must have attended him faithfully for many, many years. I fear I cannot accept them since I am unable to countenance the grief it must cause him to part from them after such long service. Moreover, since they will serve as examples of the populace of Banjarmasin to the great *Tuan* Raffles who sent me here, when next I meet him, it might be better to constitute a fresher assemblage of younger and more attractive persons who may cultivate a more accurate picture in his mind of the vigour and energy of the sultan himself.'

The chamberlain stared, wild eyed. He had got the vinegar beneath all that honey all right. This was not possible. To refuse the sultan's gift. It would be counted his fault. He would be punished, perhaps even stripped of his office.

'*Tuan* Hare, I cannot … It is not seemly that …'

Hare pursed his lips. Time to wave the shadow of British cannon over him. 'Pray tell His Majesty this, since I am so mindful of his serene happiness and would not, for the world, distress him by a selfish acceptance. Since any gift to me is also a gift to *Tuan* Raffles, I am sure he would not wish to cause *him* distress also.'

It was eleven o' clock in the morning. At two in the afternoon, the chamberlain returned to Hare's house, all hand-twisting eagerness, wiping the sweat from his brow, tripping over his own slippers at the door. This time, he had brought a troop of street urchins, hastily deloused and scrubbed up to be full of white-toothed, smiling winsomeness. They marched in mock-militarily, stood in line and giggled, excited by this novelty of seeing a white man, nudging each other in a puppyish playfulness that would have melted any heart. Hare sent them off with a flea in their ear. If he wanted children, he could beget more of his own.

By five o' clock the sultan had finally understood. Hare was accorded the ultimate honour of dining on the crumbs from under the royal table and presented with two beguiling *houris* who peered coyly through diaphanous headscarves and sent out thick waves of perfume that beat on the humid air. Their distended, dangling earlobes betrayed their ultimate forest origins. The mark of savagery excited him. Perhaps they were ex-palace but spoke no form of Malay that he had access to as wild things brought in from the woods. But their jangling bangles would replace words and, after all, silent women were the best kind. The smooth, golden flesh of their wrists and ankles inflamed him, the sweet, contrasting pinkness of their toenails, dark eyes, bee-stung lips, slim, swaying gait began an itch that must soon be scratched. Their bodies would be hard and spiced, full of delicious textures and tastes, not blandly soft like the uncooked pastry of Western women. Their breath in his face would be heavy with all the rich aromatics of the East.

Hare welcomed them with a bow, swallowed hard to calm the blood raging in his ears and ordered them to be sent down to the farm on the huge tract of land the sultan had granted him as his personal domain, to await his pleasure – Christmas presents to be unwrapped only after excited and leisurely anticipation. After all, it had been pointed out that it would be rude to send them back again, an affront to local custom. Strictly speaking, it might be thought proper to pass the girls on to his superior in Batavia but poor old Raffles would only be embarrassed and stare at his boots and not know what to do with them and that would be enough to drive his wife back on the bottle and make his life hell again. Poor old Tom Raffles was an indecently decent man. Best spare everyone the bother. When in Rome, do as Caligula; in Banjarmasin, as the sultan does. It was truly extraordinary the things a man was required to do in the loyal service of a grateful nation.

***

Yes, Arthur Grimes felt sure that was pretty much how it must have been. The British were beginning to feel their oats after their 1811 invasion of Java to stop the French using it as a naval base to disrupt their trade with China. Early domino theory. A pub game guides an empire's foreign policy and there is no such thing as a new idea. The duty levied on China tea paid for the huge British Navy but, without the China Trade, would they ever have needed the navy in the first place? No one was permitted to have that thought. Raffles, the young British Lieutenant-Governor, was a shiny, new broom aiming to sweep clean without getting his bristles too dirty. He owed Hare a favour for helping prepare the Java campaign with intelligence on local conditions and so sent him to a well-paid post in Borneo, the declared aim to help the sultan in the suppression of pirates. But everyone knew that it was the Dutch monopoly that drove honest seamen to piracy in the first place and that the rulers themselves took a hefty cut in the profits. Hare had lost ships to piracy himself but Arthur had no doubt he was really there just to further muddy the soupy waters, to sign treaties on the East India Company's behalf that would still stand firm if and when the Dutch came back and so undermine their claims to the entire region. And the whole war was run by the Company before governments had learnt the importance of keeping grubby commercial enterprises out of public affairs as they did nowadays.

Arthur put down his pen and glasses and rubbed his grainy eyes and chomped contentedly on the sausage roll on his desk, spooning up the last gob of ketchup in a cusp of crisp pastry, dropping a blob on his papers. Bok would be annoyed if it spoiled his dinner. Arthur knew pretty much all there was to know about Alexander Hare. In libraries, the Farquhar Museum where he worked and his study off Singapore's Orchard Road, he had chewed through the archives with ferreting, scholarly resolve and gathered together all the documents relating to that extraordinary figure, described by Stamford Raffles' second wife, with sweet-tongued venom, as 'the eccentric Mr. Hare'. Arthur had physically retraced the Hare family's footsteps from London's Bedford Square, across Asia by land and sea, through sand and swamp to India, slept where they had slept and looked on the blasted ruins of their various houses with suitable Ozymandian poignancy. His pride and joy was the great clock in the living room, bought at crippling cost from an auction house in India, whose dial read 'Alexander Hare, clockmaker of Grevill Street, London, 1794', etched in silver on a brass face – built by Hare's own father. They were a family that acted as if names cost money and must be handed down like old pullovers from generation to generation regardless of fit.

Through the long years of Japanese imprisonment during the war, he had thumbed those papers nightly in his head and dreamed through them in hot mosquito-ridden visions tossed on a bed of raw concrete. Denied pencil and paper as a capital offence, Arthur had written ghostly notes on the foetid night-time air and, as his blood was sucked and insidious fever infused into his boiling brain, he felt he had slowly entered Hare's mind. Or perhaps it was that Hare had entered his. Free will was an obvious but possibly necessary fiction. Sometimes, he thought he was haunted.

No statues would ever be raised up to Alexander Hare like that to Raffles down by Singapore harbour – like *those* to Raffles – since an all-white one had been commissioned to correct the shocking suggestion of brown skin conveyed by the original bronze. Hare's was a character too close to the unvarnished truth about what men were and what they wanted, to offer himself as a vessel to be filled with the noble justifications and sweeping ideals that statuary demands. You don't build statues to cautionary tales. His crime was that of revealing us to ourselves and people don't like it when you tell them what they already know and that's the whole of Freud right there. It wasn't a pretty sight and it wouldn't be forgiven or turned into a morally uplifting conclusion. Freud had never had to ask, 'What is it that men want?' Being one himself, he already knew.

Arthur had never seen an image of Hare, probably none existed. Why would it? Hare had left no becalmed, pining sweetheart behind in chilly London, just a set of no-nonsense brothers, quill-sucking over their accounts, who had founded the portentous-sounding House of Hare to trade to the East. In 1820, a woman calling herself Johanna van Hare, would petition to be confirmed in the Church in Malacca, declaring herself 'no longer' the concubine of Alexander. Presumably she was a Mardijker, of freed slave descent. Racial terms seldom meant what they said. Most of the 'Dutch' of Malacca were Eurasian and most of the 'Portuguese' the outpourings of Indian clerks from Goa. Come to think of it, Hare had previously traded in both Portugal and India, so anything was possible. The original letter is in Dutch – Malacca being at the time a Dutch possession – but has had to be written for her since she is reduced at the end to making her illiterate mark. What language did they speak together, she and Hare? Dutch? Portuguese? Hindi? Malay? Hare would have had a smattering of them all but then he probably never went in for much conversation within the household. Johanna was – again presumably – the mother of those children that he acknowledged, his brood of leverets. And what language did he speak with the other bed-partners? People somehow could never see past the sex but that left everything else unexplored. Was Hare remote or friendly? How did he fill those sudden, long, empty hours of awkward marital proximity that had been revealed to Arthur on his honeymoon?

No image for Johanna then. But somehow those sleepless nights in Changi had beckoned forth in Arthur's mind a clear, contemporary kitkat portrait of Hare in a gilded frame – perhaps by Chinnery with lots of his trademark piquant, red highlights on nose and eyes. He saw Hare as of middling height, fair-haired, good-looking enough but his real attractiveness lay in his sparkling charm and a firm, assertive but not unfriendly manner – a man comfortable in his own skin – that most desirable of qualities that cast a sort of glow about him. Arthur had never felt that. The eyes must surely have been blue, something that exerts a fascination in the East but not without worrying overtones of madness, an impression that would have been reinforced by his bold gaze staring out of the canvas at the viewer, with raised chin. And in the background there would have been the waving palm trees or spouting volcanoes that showed his exotic location, while by his side an image of whatever he considered his greatest triumph. In his own portrait, Stamford Raffles had set his book, *The History of Java*, there in full authorial vanity and a scatter of Javanese antiquities as part of his claim that Java was one of the great civilisations of the world and therefore deserved the ultimate accolade of permanent inclusion in the British Empire. What might have been Hare's choice? A difficult question, for, to sum up, Alexander Hare was what ever-angry youth would call a sexist, racist, colonialist rapist that everyone found to be a thoroughly delightful fellow – though perhaps a bit of a dog.

Writers, Arthur knew, are often hounded by devoted readers who want to know about their private lives because they have been inside their heads and feel they own *them*. Like jealous spouses, they resent any reservation, anything withheld, and seek to pluck some extra and neglected sliver of truth from their bones not contained within the slim covers of their works. But writers put all their creativity and insight, anything about themselves that is worthwhile and unique, into their books so that they always disappoint in the flesh by their numbing ordinariness. Writers themselves are sucked oranges, no juice left, just discarded pips and peel. More interesting for Arthur, was to ask what book Hare, whose own life was so colourful, might have written had he been so inclined – Hare's apocrypha – and there were haunting signs of such an inclination.

The British Museum contained Hare's diary, presented in 1903 by someone who was presumably a descendant of the Batavia shipping agent who had received it in 1854. But then perhaps not. Arthur had laboured through it, the last time he had passed through London, after the war, working his passage home as medical officer on a tanker, hoping it would reveal all. Diaries are the laundry baskets of our lives. It is there you find our dirty underwear, the slops and stains and inadvertent admissions and emissions of mouth, crotch and armpit, thoughtlessly tossed and revealing the truths we seek to launder from the outside world. At the very least they retain a lingering stale whiff of the true self. But this was a curious document, a copy of a purloined copy made secretly by an enemy, bought for money and of doubtful provenance and liberally amended with furious rancour by the man who sought, above all others, to be Hare's nemesis and destroy him. The parts supposed to be by Hare himself were more about posturing in a mirror than intimate revelation. Sometimes it was almost as if Hare saw a biographer coming from afar and moved to deliberately checkmate him in advance. He was man who loved to set other hares running.

Much of the diary was gibberish or illegible in its careworn ink on blotched pages. It had been circulated with the explicit intention of blackening Hare's name around the world and bringing him down so perhaps it had passed through many excited hands in Asia and Europe or perhaps it had been so uninteresting to the world that it had lain neglected in the leaky downstairs lavatory of a country house for generations. It was as trustworthy as a three-pound note and its hushed preservation in fluffed, acid-free tissue in controlled library humidity seemed like a deliberate irony, like a lethal scorpion specimen at his own museum, nested in caring cotton wool. As a specimen, it could mean anything or nothing but the sting was still to be avoided. Arthur had laughed out loud at the conceit and been silently shushed by reading room glares. And the purging of the last war had ensured there would be no undiscovered cache of letters to be found in the drawers of some old cabinet in Jakarta or Eastcheap. The application for confirmation by Johanna van Hare of Malacca said she was trying to learn Malay and making a pig's ear of it so not a fertile basis for amorous correspondence. There would be no need of a prune-faced wife to burn Hare's awkward, post mortem letters such as Captain Cook and Richard Burton had. Arthur looked off into the distance and daydreamed.

***

The carriage deposited Alexander Hare before the main door of the Buitenzorg palace, a white façade of imperial, puffed-up periwiggery, with a servant's elegantly gloved hands unlatching the door. A landau would have been better, for what could be more agreeable than to ride at speed in an open coach through a tropical night of warm, fragrant breezes and dancing fireflies with the horses' hooves striking the odd spark from the stones of the shaded Great Post Road? But Buitenzorg was too close to the mountains so that rain was a constant threat and a closed carriage it had to be. The Dutch were a pain with their endless rules about who could wear a sword, or diamonds, or carry an umbrella or have glass in their carriage windows and insisted on the local people, seated by the roadside, rising and baring their heads or descending from horseback to acknowledge their greatness. The British had let such humiliations lapse which was as much a relief to the passenger as the locals. The French puppet Daendels had built that road across Java with forced labour at the cost of God knew how many Javanese lives and now its slow deterioration under the British was a source of great head-nodding satisfaction to Dutch patriots.

It had been a long journey up from the capital and Hare reached up and tipped the sweating Javanese coachman generously. Good politics. Always remember the little people. If you want to make friends with a man, first make friends with his dog. The man touched his whip to his *blangkon* headdress in acknowledgement and rattled away happily over the cobbled yard, teeth shining in the dark. Javanese had very pretty teeth, small and comely, not like Hare's own great dental tombstones but the upper classes liked them fashionably blackened, holding a man with white teeth to look too much like a monkey. Hare liked to make people happy but not at the cost of his teeth.

The Lieutenant Governor's cool mountain retreat, forty-odd

miles from steamy Batavia, was bathed in golden light – candles within, flickering bamboo torches without – decorated for the king's birthday, everything reflecting off the shimmering light of the pond. Like its name, Buitenzorg was a lumpish Dutch version of airy Sanssouci, with slim rococo replaced by a rather grim and dumpy classicism, a swallow transformed into a dodo, but then the architect of Sanssouci was Dutch so perhaps no inferences concerning national character should be drawn. Anyway, it all looked well enough to Alexander Hare, a watchmaker's son from the pinched houses of Hatton Garden.

At that point in his life, Hare had always liked the Dutch, a steady people yet one given to endearing fits of giddiness that redeemed them. The Dutch did not greatly like the British whom they thought to have been thrust upon them by their foolish, exiled Stadholder and whose future intentions they held suspect. Once Napoleon had been driven out of Holland, would they really ever want to give back the jewel that was Java? The Dutch rather thought not and were right in that belief. And, even if the British did so, ever after they would know that they held on to the Indies only on British sufferance. Any time he wanted, that dreadful man Raffles could come back, swinging his axe at their love of monopolies and domestic slavery, the whole basis of colonial order. Mr. Raffles could be a bit of a bore about slavery. His father had been in the West Indies trade as a ship's master and they had not got on, so that it became a bone of contention between them. The gardeners at Buitenzorg were slaves too, of course, but they were part of the emblem of the Dutch establishment that could not be tampered with on pain of upsetting the touchy Batavians.

So, instead of freeing them, Raffles had used them to transform the fussy gardens into something after the more informal English style where untamed streams now cascaded over immemorial rocks instead of spouting from the mouths of strangulated stone fish. In place of restored freedom, they were given the illusion of Nature. Up here, you could draw invigorating, almost English air, into your lungs.

'Mr. Sikandar Hare!' An Indian flunky in full fig velvet, called out the name to the assembly and handed back the invitation card with both hands. Hare had to smile. To the British, The East Indies were 'this other India', run from Calcutta and to be understood in Indian terms, Java a mere minor deviation from the mainland model which might be used to correct that deviation. The flunky was returning the compliment to the Graeco-Roman world. Sikandar indeed! From the back of the ballroom, a military orchestra with an excessively drumbeat sense of rhythm and augmented by a couple of stringed instruments, was wrestling with popular airs, pounding and chopping them into march tunes to be served up by numbers. The local *gamelan* percussion orchestra that Mr. Raffles kept playing to establish his equivalence with a traditional raja was quieted and packed away for the day. What Mr. Raffles did with native airs, Hare did with his ladies. The possession of a seraglio was another way of speaking the native tongue and slightly easier on the ears.

The main salon blazed with a dozen crystal chandeliers and was crowded with the British and their ladies – all shooshed up and preened in best bib and tucker. Scarlet uniforms, gold epaulets, gleaming leather and diamond pins for the men, silk, feathers and flashing jewels of every hue for the ladies, fluttering their fans and twittering like birds of paradise. Men outnumbered women, naturally. This was still a military establishment and many of the soldiers had entered into local domestic arrangements that were of a strictly private nature and not for public display. At the far end, stood Mr. Raffles in muted civilian dress, a touch of autumn browns in a bed of raging summer flowers, surrounded by his clique of ambitious, nice young men, enthusiastic puppies, all wagging their tails before the top dog. Having come a long way from humble origins himself, Hare could recognise the marks of travel on others who held themselves to be moving upstream. There was no need for all this personal ostentation of dress. At Malacca, when the British expeditionary force arrived, the natives had been most impressed by a huge Indian bass drummer with twirled moustaches flaunting a leopard-skin tabard but were stunned to silence when Lord Minto, Governor General of India, an easy aristocrat, had disembarked onto the dock from the East India Company flagship, before the whole, glorious invasion army and fleet, a tiny, bent figure in hushed black who spoke so softly that you had to lean forward to catch his words. It seemed that all that crowd of beautiful uniforms of scarlet and gold bowed before him as bobbing parrots and flamingos before a humble crow. Hare, himself, could never fawn like that, having a healthy independence of mind and conduct.

He looked around carefully. Mrs. Raffles in watered silk was surrounded by Company wives, ever so queeny, favouring them with her views and knocking back the unwatered brandy as usual. Tomorrow they would all be bitching behind her back as they had at Penang from where the Indian scandal of a child born out of wedlock had followed her here. By the window, a group of worried-looking men like undertakers were rasping in phlegmy Dutch through cigars, ignoring the presence of ladies and knocking back orange bitters and *kirschwasser*. Later they would scratch up a game of whist. There would be few Dutch tonight, just those men from the Ruling Council who had the wisdom to see the British occupation as an opportunity or at least something to be lived with. Inevitably, they would later be sneered at as collaborators, despite the co-operation of the Dutch government in exile with the current administration.

**

Arthur paused. Co-operation. Collaboration. What a fine line there was between the words but what a difference between the two.

It was broad daylight and he looked out through the museum window through shading palm fronds. A worker was hosing down the forecourt, giggling and threatening to soak a man selling noodles at the gate. The noodle-seller was laughing back and menacing the worker with his wheeled cart so that a sort of joke oriental bullfight was in the offing. They were both so taken over by sheer joy that they could hardly stand. How was it possible to get so much pure pleasure out of doing two crappy jobs? When had he himself become so incapable of simple happiness? He turned back to the room, grumpily puzzled.

At the Farquhar Museum, his office was an eccentric structure, as all museum offices are, under constant pressure of space, jostled by nesting oddments from the bird collections, duplicate periodicals and camera lenses blinded with dust. After the years of imprisonment under the Japanese, it still felt strange to be surrounded by so many *things*, just lying about, not pocketed up, stripped down, reapplied, traded, everything made valuable through scarcity.

Arthur looked down at the old, fat Swan fountain pen he still used, its Bakelite casing grown matt and scratched with age. When released from Changi back then, he had wandered pointlessly in the gutted, ruined city, incapable of *feeling* the change but had returned like a homing pigeon to the museum and been shocked to see Japanese soldiers still casually in charge. The Allies had few forces available to make their surrender a reality. Japanese troops had had to police their own official acceptance of defeat at City Hall. They might have had to surrender to themselves if Mountbatten hadn't rushed in and been so keen to get in front of a camera and show off his profile and, in an upper-class drawl with Mayfair rolled 'r's, accuse the Japanese of *rrrejcial errrogence* as if a great shoulderload of exactly that was not what made up the white man's burden. Empire and democracy, after all, were only compatible behind a screen of racism. In the newsreels, they always used the same background music of falling cadences for Japanese that they used for Red Indians in westerns. He had never understood why. Perhaps the implication was that both spoke with forked tongue.

How many nights had he plotted this moment when he would be free to smash the faces of his tormentors, kick their whimpering bodies – 'Banzai you bastards!', pay his torturers back in vicious tit for all the quite unnecessary tat he had suffered, ping for their pong! Now, the sight of them evoked in him not the expected hatred and urge for revenge so much as an overwhelming sense of embarrassment. Arthur looked at the young sentry, still a complete set with rifle and bayonet, who looked back at him in his newly issued shorts – made to fit the man he once had been and so comedically baggy for the emaciated wreck he now was. Arthur walked straight at him, dismissing him as an illusion, so that the soldier gave one terrified look at this walking corpse and ducked to one side to let him pass, 'Aiiih!' dropping his rifle with a clatter.

Arthur passed on unchallenged, invisible, immaterial, noting everywhere neglect and decay. The entry hall still snarled with Japanese ideograms and flags, celebrating serial victories and an unstoppable future. Then a curatorial reflex kicked in. They should collect that Union Jack, the one Mountbatten had run up on the Padang, the only one secretly kept in Changi after that buffoon Percival had refused to parade with it alongside a white flag when *he* surrendered. People often cared more for the symbols of things than the things themselves. At that moment, anyway, he was heartily sick of people. Things were more reliable. The galleries were dusty and full of broken glass that he avoided in his careworn sandals and he made for his old office, *this* office. Stuffed birds on branches wall-eyed silently from their cases. Arthur opened the door and surprised a Japanese officer, leaning back in a chair – *his* chair – feet on the desk, peacefully smoking a cigarette and looking down at a black, shiny handgun in front of him. Despite the hateful uniform and the razored haircut, he had the chubby face of a Renaissance cherub and should have been swirling on a ceiling above the heads of lubricious popes. They contemplated each other in silence.

'Come in and sit down, old man. I was sort of expecting you. Don't worry. I'm not thinking of shooting either myself or you. Just tired of carrying this great, heavy thing around. You look a little tired too. I like your beard by the way. Very lush. That's one thing we rising sons can't do as well though our chaps up north can – the Hairy Ainu, you know.' Perfectly accented English. An elegant drawl worthy of Lord Louis Mountbatten himself. Arthur went in and took a dusty seat. They clearly didn't get a lot of visitors here or cleaners. It had become an Alice in Wonderland world. The Mad Hatter would turn up soon and offer him tea.

'Your English. It's so … English.'

'Cambridge, old man. Three years at Jesus undergoing the rigours of Eng. Lit. according to the great Quiller-Couch before I joined up. That's why they sent me here. But it leaves scars.' He swung his legs back to the floor. 'Take a smoke?' Cigarettes offered from an exquisitely carved sandalwood box that he recognised as an item inappropriately appropriated from the collection. A lighter flared with hand-held politeness. 'I take it you have some sort of official link with this place?' He waved a hand airily. 'Take your word for it.' He ran an amused smile over the shorts. 'Can't exactly ask for documentation, I suppose? Thought not. The important thing is for me to hand over the twigs and stuffed birds officially so I can go back to barracks with a clean slate and nip back to dear old Nippon as and when. Now, what I need from you is some sort of a signature on this chit.' He reached into a breast pocket and handed over an old Swan fountain pen, pushed two pieces of paper across the table, covered with ideographic scuttling spiders. 'Just a receipt. Afraid it's all in Japanese but I'll leave you the copy so you can get your chaps to translate it. I'll throw in the gun and the pen free like they did at City Hall.' He stretched and yawned extravagantly and got to his feet.

Arthur would not have been surprised to hear him say a farewell 'Toodle-pip'. He signed awkwardly, fingers a little stiff and unwilling, as if signing a receipt for the whole war. He had not written anything in years. The Japanese shot you for keeping notes. 'You seem to be taking the Japanese defeat rather well.'

'War's not really my thing, old man.' He mouthed distaste as if at bad port at high table. 'Same for you by the look of things. Changi was it? Your colleagues, the "co-operators" have all cleared off to the Botanical Gardens and dug in there, keeping their heads down. Have to cultivate our garden and all that. I don't suppose they're looking forward to what you might have to say to them when you get back from durance vile. They had a chit too, from the old British governor, saying they could stay *en poste*.' He grinned naughtily. 'Hope for their sake they kept it.'

'What will you do back home?' They were talking like old friends. The chaos had swept away all sense of hierarchy and structure. They were two human beings bumping into each other on the moon.

'Oh, rest up for a bit and then finish my novel. Time for some deep Kafkaesque themes of solitude and alienation in Japanese literature, I think. Don't know Kafka? Oh, you really should.

He captures the essential, bureaucratic alienation of our age.' He pocketed the chit and buttoned down the flap. 'Every time I look at the stuffed jackdaw out there, it seems to be nagging me. Kafka's dad used one – a *kavka* – as his business logo in the fashion trade. So perhaps this war can be turned into something worthwhile – ill winds and atom bombs and so on.'

Arthur inhaled on the cigarette and choked. It tasted of bombed-out, burning buildings. Another habit lost in the camp. He longed for his pipe, a real smoke, yearned to cradle the bowl like a warm scrotum. Then he looked round the room, fully taking in the devastation for the first time. 'What happened to the stuff stored here? In particular a green, steel trunk with my name on it, Arthur Grimsby. It contained my research notes on Alexander Hare, my birds survey, a manuscript I was working on, all my photos of the Cocos-Keeling Islands...'

The officer sucked his teeth in dental regret. 'Oh dear. Photos? Your kit was it? Ah yes. Well, I'm afraid the secret intelligence Johnnies took all that away. Cocos-Keeling, you see. It was going to be the next stepping-stone in our glorious march to Australia and world domination, old chap. Photos of beaches were worth their weight in gold. They got very excited when they found it. Your name on the lid? Surprised they didn't come and look you up in Changi.' He chuckled. 'Rather lucky for you though.'

Arthur leapt to his feet, dithering, pale, mouth agape. The room span. 'All gone? And my manuscript, what of that?' he wailed.

'Oh, the rest they used to sell off for wrapping paper in the market, one of their little perks. You can't begrudge it to them really. We lost quite a lot of the periodical back numbers that way but their paper was glossy, you see, so not as good for wrapping fish as your documents. Yours was far more absorbent if not absorbing. I even think I saw some of your stuff being used to bundle up those syrupy caramel sweets the Indians do.' He pincered theatrically sticky finger and thumb and popped them lusciously in his mouth as Arthur collapsed with his head in his hands – the years of work so lightly destroyed, the dashed anticipation of being reunited with a purpose greater than mere brute survival and a bridge to the future! Tears streamed down the emaciated face, the tears he had reached for but been unable to cry till now for all the loss and pain and despair of the past few years, now shed for a few bits of paper in an old trunk that no one else cared about. He wailed aloud like a baby, beyond shame. Great sobs shook his skinny bones. Snot dribbled from both nostrils. Yet, at the same time, Arthur observed himself from without with the piqued interest of a dispassionate scientist. Who could have thought there was so much moisture to be squeezed from such an arid carcass as his own?

'There, there. Don't upset yourself, old chap.' The officer yawned with world-weariness and stretched his arms. 'It's only paper and at least it shows people were wrong if they said you couldn't write for toffee.'

***

'Mr. Raffles.' Hare gave him one of his professional smiles, clasped both hands together before his crotch and nodded a penguin's bow before his benefactor. The acolytes turned and gave him hard stares, their eyelids sash windows slamming down on a street urchin's impertinent fingers. Raffles was younger than Hare, short, floppy-haired, stooped as a pecking hen but gimlet-eyed as a sparrowhawk.

'Ah, Mr. Hare. Fresh from Banjarmasin?' He extended a hand, cool but firm, and placed another hand over it in blessing like a priest.

'Tonight, from my brother's house, sir, in town.'

Raffles waggled an eyebrow. 'Perhaps I should call you Sultan Hare, from what I hear. Your own native palace where you sit in native dress with full local perquisites? Your very own fiefdom down there in Mokolo, fourteen hundred square miles and all yours by unencumbered personal right.' The young men chortled and sniggered but pricked up their ears at the sound of another's advancement. 'Yes, I have cleared it with Calcutta. There will be no problem there. The estate is yours, unentailed, with no claim upon it by the Company. And I must congratulate you on your efforts with the other sultan of Banjarmasin. Thanks to your vigilance and the occasional showing of the flag by our naval vessels, piracy has decreased beyond all expectation and we may expect a surge in legitimate trade and a future of unlimited possibilities opens up to us.'

He was quoting something. Hare could see him in his mind's eye, sitting at his desk, fluffing up the rosy news for Calcutta in flowery prose – plans, estimates, predictions – all filigree spun out of a chance remark or nothing at all and fixed onto paper with his quivering quill like some fortune teller who sees a chip in his crystal ball as the portent of a whole new world order. Raffles was a man for whom being English was not just a postal address but a destiny. Hare had no illusions about the effectiveness of his own activities in Borneo. It would turn out that there had been some domestic squabble among the pirates and they had been busy killing each other instead of Company sailors or perhaps slave-raids were more profitable this year than seized spice that was a glut on the market. It was all politics, turning wheels within wheels.

'And consumption of opium, sir, is up by twenty chests ...'

A cloud passed over Raffles' face. The Company would be pleased. It meant more revenue to counter the unbroken stream of silver they were pouring into Java and would look good in a report. But he hated the idea of the drug and its predatory effects on his Javanese.

'... mainly for the coastal Chinese of course.' The cloud lifted again. 'But I have a plan – far from hare-brained – I should like to lay before you when you have a moment's leisure.'

The young men stiffened. It seemed to Hare that they silently closed ranks around Raffles, like brothers around an heiress at the soft, approaching tread of a gold-digging suitor. Or perhaps it was like schoolchildren huddling around their teacher at the sudden sight of a large and frightening dog. Either way, it was clear that they were true believers in the gospel of Raffles. Young men make bad mercenaries. They need a cause and in Raffles they had one.

Money! It was always the boss's weak point. Raffles had no head for it. He secretly prided himself on his unworldliness. Cash flowed through his fingers and he spent it like water – building the Harmonie club, reorganising the palace, snapping up old manuscripts and clogging up the Company's ships with animal specimens for the museum back home in Leadenhall Street. He had sent a bloody great elephant all the way to Japan for God's sake, as a present for the shogun! As it turned out, they couldn't get it off the ship. There were no docks and though elephants can swim, they cannot *dive* and it had been politely returned to sender. While the Calcutta Presidency and the Directors back in London howled and waved balance sheets, he saw himself as some great Company entrepreneur but that was just one of the visions to which he was prone – he was very good at visions. Raffles was surely the world's worst business man – a nervous racehorse hitched to a drayman's cart – and his aides tried to save him from himself, not by direct confrontation, which he took badly, but by forgetting, misunderstanding, toning down as a good wife might her husband. Hare could imagine them at breakfast, chewing on their lamb chops, dreading the moment when he entered the room, full of bounce, waving the sheaf of papers in which he had recorded his latest visions of the night – ban the use of judicial torture in all the law courts, write the book of traffic regulations afresh, replace the entire system of taxation in a manner that required compiling a very Doomsday Book of the whole island of Java, forbid the further importation of slaves. He could picture the subservient smiles and nodding at the boss from around the table and the exchanges of eye-rolling and groans among themselves. It would all make endless work in what could otherwise have been a nice, cosy sinecure with lots of time for drinking and pig-sticking and chasing women and would annoy the Dutch as a sign the

British were here to stay. A man who borrows another's house just for a couple of weeks does not normally begin by knocking down the front wall and redesigning the garden.

Travers, Raffles' *aide-de-camp*, was swiftly there with a hand under Hare's elbow steering him away like an importuning drunk. More petitions? More work? More expense? Not if he could help it.

'If you would but submit your detailed plan to me in writing, fully costed in several copies, *together with your overdue accounts*, we should surely give it due consideration, Mr. Hare.' Travers' eyes glared into Hare's. The plan would naturally go straight into a bin somewhere.

'Of course.'

Travers relaxed his grip, turned back – he had a nasty boil on the back of his neck, a little Javanese volcano of his very own – and as he turned Hare was through the gap like a rat up a drain, pulling a roll of proposals from his inner pocket and sliding them into Raffles' hands. 'I foresaw the urgency of a written outline, sir, and am glad to oblige.'

Raffles sighed and clutched it to his bosom. 'I will read it, Mr Hare. You have my word.'

Hare was satisfied. Raffles was a renowned swot and would be going back to his desk with relief as soon as the guests hit the road. Heat and sullen rage radiated from the wrong-footed puppies. Travers picked angrily at his boil and glared. Too bad.

Hare took his leave, bowing away from the group and flicked his fingers at a servant to summon a glass of Champagne. Job done, he could relax. He passed out into the garden, firm stone underfoot, then gravel, then grass, a little refreshing rain in the wind perhaps and lightning growling over the mountain. Beyond the railings, in the woven native huts, little fires could be seen burning like glowworms. Later there would be fireworks, wheeing and farting up into the night sky but at present the lake was peaceful, the swans bedded down, trying to grow back enough left wing-feathers to supply ever-scribbling, quill-plucking Raffles. Inside, the sweating bandmaster raised his baton to the men in their soaked tunics and struck up again and a nasty rash of dancing broke out to reeling Scottish whoops and the crash of boots, stamping out their exaggerated, strutting manhoods.

Hare loathed Scottish dancing. But there was no shortage of Scots in the Company. Of course, Hare's own parents called themselves Scotch and it was a card he had occasionally played himself to gain advantage. After a while, the music changed and the background blur of noise gelled into clarity and he recognised the popular jig, 'Money in Both Pockets', played with lots of energetic fiddling. How apt.

***

Arthur had always wondered about Olivia Raffles. In the literature there were two firmly held and totally incompatible views of her – chaste and dutiful partner or brandy-guzzling slapper – and, surely, no way to build a bridge between them. Or was it possible to see the same woman in two such contrasting ways? Perhaps a stern morality that had damned mere girlish foibles out of hand and forced her into the more general mould of a stage villainess, obscuring any lack of fit, might do it. There was plenty to make British Indian society hold its nose. She was a widow, older than her husband, illegitimate, had had an affair on the boat out to India and borne the captain a bastard daughter, rumours surrounded her relationships with poets – always a doubtful breed – and she was of 'Circassian' descent. Circassian women were held to be the principal denizens of the Ottoman and Persian harems and featured heavily in the fevered dreams of young ensigns so that it was small wonder that she was named as the inspiration of the erotically charged poems of Anacreon Moore.

Arthur did not really miss his own wife and she inspired in him no urge to erotic versification. Her death had been sudden and unexpected, just a couple of months before and he could argue that he was still in shock, the impact still feeding through his system. Or perhaps it was just that, as you got older, it became increasingly hard to feel strong emotion of any kind from a sort of furring up of the nerves. He doubted he would ever bother to have sex again and had ceased to think of himself as a sexual being. It was surely just another stage he had grown through and out of, for it was only after a certain age that you realised what an effort it all was and began to doubt whether it was worth it at all. He and Eileen had married young, mere students, in an icy college chapel and, as is so often the way, grown apart rather than together. They had been in love with the idea of being in love more than with each other. As far as the ceremony was concerned, his chief memories were of the atmospheric chill and the chaplain finding it impossible to remember their names. That might have been seen as an omen – more appropriate for a funeral than a wedding – but neither of them had as yet experienced that overinterpretation of the random that is the way of the East. Eileen was in her first year, Arthur a post-grad but she was the responsible adult and had shrugged on a white coat and plodded her way up to a senior position as a hospital coroner along a well-trodden and clearly marked path. Arthur's own career had been less regular and more a matter of snakes and ladders, or rather birds and ladders. The medical degree he had undergone was a mere sop to his father and reflected neither his own interests nor his intentions. Like Hare, Arthur was by nature a collector. A hoarder.

As a child, his bedroom had been littered with birds' eggs, fossils, stone arrow-heads dug from the chalk pits around the house. He had always felt a nervous reluctance to throw anything away. Clothes he had outgrown, shoes he had outworn, he liked to tuck away in cupboards, unconsciously curating his own life. These things were witnesses, had absorbed his essence, they had an enduring relationship and the collection had a powerful moral and emotional aspect. They had served him well, given their all and deserved gratitude and respect in retirement if not affection. It had been an early source of conflict with Eileen, a ruthless organiser and weeder-out of superfluity. She would be at home in one of those minimalist Japanese houses you saw in *National Geographic*, all bare surfaces and uncluttered, long-grained vistas. In the early days, of course, logic had been on her side as they moved through a series of boxy, rented properties that crushed and constrained. No airing space. No storage space. No breathing space. Prosperity had brought room and room had created the opportunity to hoard again. Small wonder that one of Arthur's youthful fascinations had been the study of magpies that stuffed their nests with bright but useless geegaws.

In fact, he observed magpies carefully over the course of a whole year of mating, nest-building and youthful flocking but despite the fervid testimony of folklore and opera, found no evidence whatever of an attraction to shiny objects amongst these maligned birds, no thieving of rings and earrings. They were actually startled and frightened by glitter and a string of bottle-tops would keep them off fields as efficiently as gunshots. Moving to Asia, Arthur switched his affections to the black kite, beloved of British squaddies for its opportunistic scavenging and so a suitable image for themselves and nicknamed with subaltern insight 'shitehawks'. And it was an article on these and their use of white scrap paper to ornament their nests and mark their status that attracted the attention of the museum and allowed him to move sideways from the medical service into it. He knew at once that he had come home, found his true nest, and began to write white academic papers to decorate the walls and gain status like a true shitehawk.

Had he loved Eileen? Yes, of course. But the word 'love' is capable of so many meanings that to say that is to say nothing. He loved his dog, he loved his job, he loved Hainanese chicken rice. At the beginning, before the wedding, there had been physical excitement that had morphed into comfort and companionship over the years, matching the rate at which the bedsprings lost their resilience and the mattress began to sag. He remembered the really big surprise of marriage to be the discovery that women snored and farted in bed as copiously as men. 'Why didn't you wake me?' she asked after a night of her bed-shaking death-rattles. 'Because you were asleep,' he answered and they laughed.

It was still love. The absence of children had kept them closer than most but children are something that changing affection can use to hide behind, invoking duty and sheer fatigue to mask growing habituation, so that their absence exposed every change to stark, surgical light. All right, it might not have the sharp urgency of ravening appetite. It might be a thing of muted tenderness that often went unexpressed and taken for granted. But it was still love. Thomas Raffles clearly loved Olivia though she was much older than him, a woman with a past and not the sort of wife who would help the career of a young man seeking to rise. And now, for all of them, it was all in the past tense.

***

'She's returned to Malacca. She took all her things and won't be coming back. She was quite angry. She broke a plate in the kitchen. One of the good ones too.'

'Really?'

'Well, she cracked it at least, so I had to throw it away.'

'But why?'

'Because they think cracked plates are unlucky here.'

'No, I mean why did she crack it in the first place?'

Hare's brother, David, had become a real Dutch burgher since his arrival from India, with his wide, floppy pantaloons, thin cotton shirt and the inevitable festering cheroot clamped between stained teeth, living in his hard-edged Dutch interior. He was fractious at being roused mid-siesta, standing here barefoot on the damp, red tiles of his living room. There were big high windows to let in northern Protestant light but with rose-tinted glass to mitigate the eastern sun's brilliance and, on the walls, pictures of the Dutch countryside that denied the reality of the Indies that surrounded the house. Alexander Hare found the overall effect intensely irritating, a house that reeked of empty afternoons.

'Why do you think? It must be the other women. What the hell did you expect, Alex? Surely, you didn't think she would be as sweet as a *stroopwafel,* did you? You can't have your cake and eat it.'

'You have a platitude for every occasion, brother. Johanna didn't mind. The other women meant less work for her she said, took the load off, and she enjoyed ordering them about. She was the wife. They were just concubines, she said. It brought her more prestige in the town. She knew the way it was, the way it always is out here and that she was raised to. It's not as if it's something I invented.' This was upsetting, not part of the plan at all. Johanna was the mother of his two children, though they were safely away in England, looked after by the other brother Joseph and having the Indies polished off them under the sconces of one of Bedford Square's finest houses. He didn't believe it was the concubines. She was angry because he'd sent the children away to be raised as English. She'd told him as much but he hadn't listened.

'What do you want sex-slaves for anyway? When a man has an itch that needs scratching there are available women enough in Batavia. Just take a walk round the market any night. Why have them hanging around your neck? How many have you got now? Five? Ten? For God's sake, man, you don't pay a slut for the firkytoodling. Every man knows what you reward her for is just clearing off afterwards and leaving you in peace without cloying attachment. Women come in a carriage where the devil is coachman. And what do they do? Sit around all day, not paying rent, picking their black teeth, chewing betel nut and guzzling your food? They're like those dogs in the market that roll their eyes at you, follow you home and just try to move in or perhaps those little birds on the Königsplein that hop around your feet asking for food and when you feed them they fly up into the trees and shit on your head. Don't you see, they're eating you alive? It's not a matter of morality but simply sound economy. You'd be better off doing what the Chinese do and keeping a pig to screw.'

Perhaps Hare found such an attitude shocking, demeaning, unchristian even. His brother had what he termed 'a standing arrangement' with a stolid Dutch widow two doors down. A standing arrangement sounded far from comfortable and a strain on the legs. Perhaps he even replied, 'Because the girls have feelings' but maybe it was not like that at all. He suspected, mostly, they did not have strong feelings. Sleeping with him was just a job. Were people passionate about glue-boiling? Both were messy but perfectly honourable tasks to be done with all-possible despatch and a good wash afterwards. Perhaps Hare knew *he* was the one who had feelings, a sense of responsibility towards his dependants, as expressed in his will where he sought to provide for them. But brother David had not seen that will yet. The myths of colonisation were there, not just for the colonised, but for the colonisers too. The British would always insist on believing that, deep down, their colonial subjects loved them and perhaps some really did.

Would Hare actually say 'unchristian'? Perhaps, if he used that inquisitorial word, it was out of mere convention. Their father had raised the Hare boys all to be of a sceptical frame of mind. A watchmaker himself, he was concerned with ways to make a watch work better not the existence of some supposed fellow great watchmaker in the sky, whose designs he followed in miniature as the wheels of the gigantic apparatus crushed and tore at mankind below with its indifferent cogged teeth. And at least a watch had a clear and useful purpose, to tell the time, whereas the world seemed to him devoid of one and the Christians who haunted churches and chapels and graveyards never seemed to get the chill of death out of their bones even in the tropics.

Hare groaned. 'You know that the Chinese pig thing is only a silly rumour spread by the Javanese because it's the most disgusting thing a Muslim can think of. It's childish, like the things we said about the masters at school and about school dinners. Hares have always been sacred to both Eros and Aphrodite on account of their high libido. And why, pray, are my women called mere sex-slaves while those of the local rulers are honoured concubines after the high Roman fashion? My ladies are equally concubines and well cared for. Only some of them are slaves and not all my slaves are women. I suppose you will see that as the sign that I have unnatural tastes as well.'

'If the cap fits, brother ...'

'I have a need for certainty and stability in my life. I need constancy and clarity, with my faithful people about me.'

David made a face. 'Faithful? You expect them to be faithful? Clinging to that idea, dear brother, is like a condemned man stringing himself up in his cell out of fear of being hanged on the morrow. No good will come of it. You're like a ship that can make no headway because its keel is fouled with clinging barnacles and you need your bottom given a good scraping to be free of them.'

Hare opened his mouth to retort, then grinned and let that one pass. 'You know that in trade credit is everything. A man must keep up a front, a certain lifestyle.'

'And is a front what you are keeping up, dear brother?' He shook his head wearily and sat down on a hard, comfortless chair – Dutch furniture always maintained a moral dimension. 'Enough. I have said my piece.' He pointed at another, meaning his brother should sit down and called out loudly for coffee. 'But what is this new arrangement I hear that you have with the Company?'

Hare smirked, sitting and smacking his own thighs in delight. 'It is the most favourable you can imagine, brother, the best in the world. The prisons here are full to bursting. I offer a cheap solution. Convicts are to be transported to my holdings in Borneo where they will be set to work and turned into colonists just as they are in America and as press-ganged jail-fodder are converted into the fine sailors of His Majesty's navy. The Company will pay for their transport, housing and sustenance.'

David turned and shouted again for coffee. 'And what will they produce on your plantation?'

'The possibilities are endless.' He reminded himself of Thomas Raffles in one of his visionary phases. 'I have in mind to harvest pepper, coffee, as well as salt and other goods to be sold for profit – tobacco too.' The word reminded him and he took out a gold filigree snuffbox from his pocket and offered before taking a pinch that he drew deep up each nostril with every sign of pleasure. 'Also, they will build ships with all the fine standing timber on my land that I have for nothing.'

David looked puzzled. 'Don't count your chickens before ... And what shall you do with these ships?'

Hare threw his head back and laughed, slapping his brother on the back. 'Why brother, that is the beauty of it. What do you think? I shall sell them or hire them to the Company, who meanwhile pay me for feeding and lodging the prisoners, so they can transport my convicts to Borneo and my coffee to Java.'

***

Arthur flipped gloomily through the *Straits Times*. As usual, it was all politics, all rubbish of no lasting interest or importance. Internal self-government for Singapore, independence for Malaya, federation or not, racial tension, threatened strikes, a terrorist attack in Kedah, indecisiveness from the British, recalcitrance from the Malays, outrage from the Chinese. An illegal demonstration for or against something or other had been forbidden and so advertised. Blah, blah. He yawned. But a tiny article tucked away on the inside pages caught his magpie eye. It was alleged that some variety of the drongo cuckoo had established itself and was breeding on the Cocos-Keeling Islands and stirring up the bored birdwatchers of the wireless-relaying station there. Excitement flared. Real news at last! But was this the square-tailed or the fork-tailed variety? It was not clear. There was no picture. And what species was the target of its brood parasitism? That was crucial. How could they not say? He tutted and read the piece again, carefully. No, nothing. He checked the other pages in hope of a follow-up. Again, nothing! And all the back page was wasted on a tedious article about the price of rubber. At all costs, he must have a specimen for the collection and check whether it was a new species or simply a displaced migrant.

Arthur leapt to his feet, seized the newspaper, grabbed his briefcase and slapped a floppy hat on his head, heading off to the museum with great purposeful strides. Outside, he paused. It was an overcast day, relatively cool but there was rain in the air, the first drops pattering down on the slick leaves of the garden. He disliked going by car, missing the happy buzz and chaos of the streets. The drive to and from work suggested the world was a scatter of British dots with everything that was truly Asian in between dismissed as irrelevant. Then, from the bottom of the stairs, he saw Bok Ong watching with an expressionless parchment face. Arthur always felt as if he saw right through you and he knew Bok disliked it when he walked. It lowered his *tuan's* status and so his own to see him hot and sweaty like a coolie. Intimidated, he turned back and climbed into the Morris, curled up under the house, its form a fat, comforting, sugared doughnut, and churned the engine in the soothing, somehow Surrey crickety smell of warm leatherette

***

Hare had not yet perfected his arrangement with the Company. There was yet more profit to be squeezed from it by bringing areas of the Borneo policy into line with practice at home. After a sticky start, things were going well in Borneo and he was making money hand over fist. He had persuaded Raffles of the need for further funding 'lest the great investment we have already made there should be entirely lost for a hap'o'rth of tar just when final success lies within our grasp'. It was true his other activities left little time to actually spend *there* himself but one of his ship's masters, John Ross, was licking the estate into shape – shipshape and Bristol fashion. Crops had been planted, the first vessel was on the slipway, now was the time to take the next step. He took pen and paper and began to write to Thomas Raffles.

The key to the ultimate success of their benevolent colonising project, he explained, was to turn the ungodly poor into honest, labouring families. People were driven to crime by the iniquitous Dutch system of forced deliveries and monopoly, being stripped of what little they had by native and foreign despotism that gave no incentive to work. Raffles' legal reforms meant that the numerous public torturings and executions that the Dutch so much enjoyed were no longer taking place and the prison population had soared as the result. Borneo was solving all these problems at a stroke, as had been foreseen. He looked through that and crossed out 'ungodly' and wrote in 'wayward' instead. It was time to take the next step – women. Women were the essential element of a magical transformation as a sort of moral philosopher's stone that alone could transmute base man into subject gold. The dreadful shortage of suitable women in the now-flourishing American colonies had been overcome by making it the place of settlement of prostitutes rounded up from the London streets and transported there, as they were nowadays to Australia. So street scum had become yeoman farmers and taxpayers. What had worked for the English in America and the Antipodes would work just as well for the Javanese now in Borneo and free both prisons and byways of undesirable elements. Thus, a double benefit would be secured for little additional expenditure and Raffles' administration would shine as a beacon of Enlightenment to the world. It struck all the right grace notes – benevolence, improvement, moral progress, the redemptive power of womanhood, practicality. Raffles believed in human goodness, the perfectibility of Man, and would gobble it down like a child slurping down sweetmeats.

He lay down his pen, sanded the proposal and took a toke of snuff, letting his mind wander to last night when he had entertained Ayu, the new patchouli-scented girl from Bengkulu, shy and giggling but tender and affectionate. She must have part Indian blood with those huge, dark eyes like bottomless wells though she claimed to be of noble stock, kidnapped and sold away by enemies of her father. Any man who plunged into those pools would come to himself half-drowned, panting, headshaking, like an exhausted turtle desperately crawling back up a powdery beach that trickled away to nothing under its flailing claws. This morning, it seemed possible that Bengkulu Sumatran was the language of Heaven.

***

Arthur thought it absurd to write a letter to Cable and Wireless, like sending a postcard to God, but any other form of communication would be held to be extravagantly expensive by the museum and become the subject of endless stiff and self-righteous memos from the board, endless as involving no postage and thriving on self-importance, so a letter it would have to be. As Arthur dictated a request for information concerning the drongo cuckoo to Miss Violet Loo, his secretary, he suddenly found himself wondering about her. If he could manage to imagine himself into the head of a 19th-century rakehell, why was *she* so impervious to his processes of empathy? Late thirties, hair a cowl of raven-black that disciplined rather than styled, muted makeup if she wore any at all, the sort of glasses that turned eyes into organs of disapproval rather than windows on the soul. The dress alone suggested hidden depths, business-like but with a hint of slinkiness. When she sat and adjusted her rump to accommodate the dictation pad, there was a definite rustle of suggestion between outer and inner garments that any woman would be aware of. He had never thought of her before as a woman broadcasting her femininity on all channels. Yet now he felt something in his groin akin to a primeval creature waking from hibernation, raising its snout and stirring in the ooze of a muddy swamp. Could it be that reassertion of life after bereavement that he had read about? What the hell was going on?

'Thank you, Miss Loo.'

She smiled a tight, buttoned-up smile of 'you're welcome'. When she rose and left, on legs that he now found strangely shapely, a scent of smouldering poppies lingered in the air. She had been his secretary for over five years. Why had he never noticed that before? Was that a backward glance she had tossed vampishly over her shoulder like a feather boa? What the hell *was* going on?

On his desk, there was plenty of work to be done, a tottering stack of files, some already growing dusty from the open window. He should review the consumption of milk in the tea room – there had been a steady and unexplained increase over the year – or check audited stationery supplies against projected needs but his heart was somehow just not in it. Instead, it was pounding in an unfamiliar rhythm but definitely pounding and his body felt strangely itchy. Maybe he was going down with prickly heat. Must dust himself down tonight with St. Luke's powder.

Puzzled, he stepped through into the outer office and opened the drawer of staff records – somehow reminiscent of those sliding steel drawers in the morgue – took one out, flicked through it. Miss Violet Miranda Loo. It was like looking up a museum object in the great register that revealed their origin, function, provenance. Miranda? Wasn't that a character from *The Tempest*? She was 38 years old. Married but widowed. Odd that she should make herself a Miss again. Perhaps that implied she saw herself as freshly available. No children. She lived out in Toa Payoh by the old spring and would take the long, hot bus ride in every day. He pictured her sitting on the bus with her rough shopping bag balanced on her lap and scratching her legs through the thin fabric of her dress. As an efficient woman she would know which side to sit in order to avoid direct sunlight in best 'posh' P & O fashion and call in at the market to shop in the evening before going home

– perhaps fanning herself as it jolted along, sweat trickling down the backs of her knees as the man crushed in the seat behind her breathed thick garlic fumes down her neck and over the clasp of the sad, little, gold cross she wore round it. The nape of her neck was strangely beguiling in his imagination, the flesh soft and smooth and terribly vulnerable over the fragile bone.

Arthur shook his head and went back to his desk, lit a pipe to drive away the lingering afterthought of smouldering poppies or garlic with its enfolding, honeysuckle smoke and tried to think about drongo cuckoos, a subject more likely than stationery supplies to capture a man's wandering thoughts and fire his imagination, but found himself suddenly surprised to be wondering what the experience of snuff up your nostrils was like and whether you could still buy it.

***

'A man is a man and has his needs. Every woman must accept that. Unlike us ladies, men are fatally flawed and when chastity locks horns with sin, sin always wins.' Olivia Raffles strengthened herself with an afternoon snifter, clearly much needed and tossed it back in one like a sailor, patted her lips with a dainty serviette and replaced the glass on the proffered tray with a gesture that suggested it was medicine taken with distaste. 'When they are removed from home, men find release where and when they can. Separation in marriage requires a certain amount of hypocrisy and a woman must turn a blind eye, sometimes two blind eyes and two deaf ears, to a man's doings abroad. Not,' she added swiftly, 'that I have any need to reduce the sharpness of either my vision or hearing where my own dear husband is concerned.'

The ladies hastily tutted, perished the thought and deferentially twittered away the very idea as they politely drank their tea. Themselves sharp-eyed, that was the third glass of hers they had counted and her conversation was tipping over into the bawdy. These teatime encounters were increasingly embarrassing but none of the Company wives dared miss them. If you were not there, you yourself would become the hot topic over the teapot.

'It is not the fact of Mr. Hare's being driven to such extremes by biological necessity or for his health's sake that shocks. It is his loudly and publicly declared preference for native women over white ladies or even the so-called "Dutch". He has repeatedly disdained the most advantageous offers and openly laughed about it at the Harmonie Club, lowering us all before the Hollanders.'

A shocked gasp ran like electric fluid round the room. 'Impossible!' cried Mrs. Anstruther, a stout lady in her fifties much given to fanning and public fainting. 'He is a man of wit and some fortune – though,' she tapped her nose with her fan, 'it is true that he has been seen wearing a sarong about the house and it is rumoured – but that surely merely as a measure of domestic economy – that he breaks his fast with rice.'

Mrs. Raffles bleared at her pityingly. 'Which he eats, madam, *with his fingers*!' A flunky fart-catcher bent to whisper in Mrs. Raffles' ear and served her with tea from a separate pot. The women pursed their lips and exchanged knowing looks. That would be 'strong' tea?

'But are not all those women on his concession merely

employed in farm labour?' Mrs. Anstruther looked around cannily for a convenient soft surface, preparing for the possibility of a faint and adjusted her bulk to swoon sideways.

'A mere smokescreen and – as is well known – where there is smoke there is fire. My husband informs me that Mr Hare's accounts are become a nightmare with no distinction made between the affairs of the Company and those of his personal installation and indulgences. It is not simply a matter of basic morality. It goes far beyond that. I fear,' she paused dramatically and wetted her lips like a judge before pronouncing the death sentence. 'I fear Hare has gone completely native.'

Social death. It had been said. It could not be unsaid. In that instant, a hundred doors crashed shut in Alexander Hare's face. Mrs. Anstruther uttered a grunt like a harpooned whale and toppled with practised grace, sliding her cup of unspilt tea tidily onto a side table as she tumbled.

***

'As for local rulers I treat them in every way as a sensible man does his wife, very complaisant in trifles, but immovable in matters of importance.' Joseph Collett, British Governor of Bengkulu, had said that or something very like it. A clever man, Collett, and he rose to the highest levels of the Company but was perhaps, Arthur thought, more expert in politics than in marriage.

Eileen had been what was politely termed a 'rambling rose', someone who searched for the perfect stranger, and her first tendril entwinements had come shortly after their arrival in Singapore.

Actually, of course, the stale old horticultural image immediately let her off the hook. If roses rambled, they did so gently, just looking for support while predatory, male bees buzzed busily and probed their passive flowers. But human sex was not something men did to women, often the reverse was the case. It never entered into the image that flowers wantonly pumped out perfumes and waved what were just brightly coloured reproductive organs in the wind. Let no one tell you that a husband does not know these things, does not smell them on that wind himself, see them in the eyes, feel them in the hands of the loved one. The fact that what he 'knows' may not be the case, is another matter, for there is a sense in which you may dread something so much that you actually cause it to happen. If blame was to be assigned, how much of it was Arthur's? It occurred to him that he might be incapable of enjoying love without guilt, like fish without vinegar. Of course, with passing years a man's soft parts grew stiff and the stiff parts grew soft but they had still been young then and he was far from old now. Wasn't her behaviour explicable only in terms of his own failure to make her happy? His own inadequacy? Was it his own ungrown-upness that was at fault or his lack of the power to excite?

The mortuary was a counterintuitively boisterous place, full of life and gallows humour – ricocheting off the white tile walls – that was like a return to student days, for here there was no need to maintain the onerous fictions of the medical profession – sober omniscience, sensitive concern, careful speech coming from faces composed to decent gravity. Down here, among the steel trays and the sloshing of hoses, cases became mere stiffs, so much dead meat to be sliced and flensed like dead whales. The great glugging pipes that fed and evacuated the hospital were all directed through the morgue, boosting its sense of gross physicality. And it was obvious that, every time he pushed through the morgue doors that swung loosely like those of a western saloon, the laughter died like a snuffed candle. The young Chinese assistants – excluded themselves from being candidates for her affections not by race but by age – took on a guarded look, communicated with each other in gestures and flashed glances and whispered quacks of Hokkien. The husband was an outsider from whom the boss's secrets were to be unthinkingly kept behind a dropped white-coated façade of total inscrutability. Going home in the evening to Arthur must have been like going down from university to live again with one's parents.

The first of her 'away team' had probably been the appropriately named Macclehose, the chief medical officer, a man with co-respondent's teeth and muscular legs that he displayed everywhere in embarrassing athletically cut shorts. He seemed not to realise that men only had legs as comic props in knobbly knees contests. He was a club-frequenting man, an eye-twinkler among bored, colonial wives, a head-thrown-back guffawer at risqué barroom jokes among men, a smug smoothiechops whose very stupidity would ensure he glided lightly over life immune to the sting of misfortune. He and Arthur detested each other on sight and Macclehose turned the knife by slapping him on the back at every opportunity and barking things like, 'Cheer up, old man, it may never happen,' knowing that it probably already had and that, in fact, he had made it happen himself. He had one of those consciously manly voices that made the glass in your hand vibrate, making what should be your escape into his loudspeaker. Arthur felt he would have made an excellent oleaginous candidate for the Conservative Party, all blare and false bonhomie. Run the medical service? Macclehose couldn't run a bath. God, how Arthur loathed him! That loathing, he was sure, had also been part of the inevitability of things. Only in novels was your wife unfaithful with men you really liked and respected, provoking agonising dilemmas for the author to unpick as you were led through a slippery moral maze with competing claims to love and friendship on either side and always, lurking in the shadows, the possibility of a sophisticated *ménage à trois*. People had suggested it about Raffles, his wife and the poet Leyden who was their constant companion. In reality, your hatred anticipated the fact, urged it to happen and your despising of your cuckolder made your own self-esteem plunge to that of a cockroach. The popularity of such men with women confirmed Arthur in the view that they probably deserved all the crap the world threw at them.

That it did happen, Arthur could not doubt. His cockroach antennae had begun to twitch early. There had been too many late nights at the hospital, too many whispered phone calls to an unspecified emergency, too many unexplained sightings of the CMO's blue-and-white Austin in the neighbourhood, coming the other way, as Arthur drove home. Then there was the buying of new underwear at Cold Storage and too many dance evenings at the club without him. 'Oh, don't come, Arthur. You know you hate it and you sit there and make such faces and spoil everyone else's fun.' It was true, of course, he did hate dancing. They had made you do it school, along with rugby – dancing both Scottish and ballroom – the latter being seen as the road to middleclass social advancement like playing golf. If they had taught you to drink, smoke and have sex at school, perhaps you would now hate those too. But it was more than that. Eileen believed in fun and he had never really understood fun.

When Arthur finally confronted her with his accusation – unwisely at the end of a long, tired evening with drink taken and hoping for indignant denial – she had looked at him evenly, blown cigarette smoke and said in a cool voice he had never heard before, 'What I do when I'm not with you is none of your business. You don't own me Arthur. I'm not your slave. You don't have a monopoly of me.'

Honesty is an overvalued quality. Often it means simply selfishness and impoliteness. It has a rawness about it whereas human interaction requires at least minimal cooking. She had looked at his lost, little boy face with manifest pity that cut like a knife and sat him down, bewildered, poured him another drink and taken one herself. 'Look Arthur. I'm very fond of you darling – you're a dear old thing – but our marriage was a mistake. We settled too early.' The voice was gentle but she tossed her hair defiantly as if putting the marriage behind her as easily as the hair behind her ears. Arthur suddenly noticed how long she wore it these days. When had that started? 'We were too young. The age difference was not just chronological, it was spiritual. Our marriage was based on mutual respect and warm regard and our shared fear of loneliness but that's not what young marriage is about. It's where you end up forty years later when you're looking back, pruning the roses and redecorating the grown-up kids' empty bedrooms. Young love is about knee-quivering passion and excitement and new experience that shatters the world as you know it. I've never had that ...' She viciously ground out her cigarette – whorishly red-lipsticked and brownstained – in a Works Department saucer, shockingly unintimidated by its being stamped Property of HM Government '... and I still want that.'

***

'Batavia is a dangerous place for you to be at the moment, brother.'

Alexander Hare blinked. Batavia was a dangerous place for any white man to be. Half of all new arrivals would be dead of the fever within a year, not counting the deaths of Chinese that they concealed to avoid paying funeral taxes, and most Company officers survived on the commission they levied on the effects of their dead colleagues. Since so much of the flow of Batavia's river water had been directed away from the town, the canals had become slime-filled and malodorous, either flooding the houses in the rainy season or emitting the foul stench of lethal miasma in the dry. Not yards from David's own door, the carcase of a dead horse was beached on a sandbank and pursuing an enthusiastic process of decomposition as people washed downstream of it – and the Javanese were addicted to constant washing, having no inkling of the terrible, debilitating effects of bathing on the human constitution, the water leaching away goodness and weakening the frame. Soon, the crocodiles would come, attracted upstream by the stench, and small children would be snatched as they played in the water. Added to this, the trees along the street held the foul air still and the narrow-fronted houses clamped the vaporous exhalations further into immobility. Anyone with any sense lived as far from the city as they could – as he himself did.

'We Brits are out now Napoleon's sorted. Since the raising of their flag on the 17th August, the Dutch are back in with a vengeance and that day will be forever a festival of their empire which means we have to get out now while the going's good, before they get a proper grip on things and start to look around for ways to give us grief. I'm heading back to India. They're after the collaborators and you quite particularly because of the Mokolo business. They're calling it 'The Banjarmasin Enormity' and using it to slander the whole British administration as a bunch of slavers and pimps. The Dutch! Talk about pots and kettles! At least you don't hire out your concubines to all and sundry like they do.'

Alexander Hare was uncomfortable, sitting here on the *trottoir* – like a Dutchman – in a pool of light spilling out of the open front door, sipping harsh cherry brandy that was like alcoholic toothache. True, it mitigated the stifling heat of the house but increased exposure to the poisonous miasma, especially dangerous at dusk. He swatted a mosquito and it spattered his own blood – the colour of more cherry brandy – over his shirt. A clock was ticking loudly from inside, one of their father's, like a theme for a headache.

'That matter is still unresolved. They had no legal right to seize my estate, no need to drive my people out by force. It's true, Ross, my manager, should never have provoked them by flying the Union Jack but my claim against them in the court still stands.'

He pouted. 'He'd even built a canal. I thought the Dutch liked canals.'

David drew on his pipe and blew smoke into the mosquitoes, removed a speck of tobacco from his tongue and stared at it on his finger as though it were a message from the gods. 'Cut your losses. Put your property in the name of your son or they'll come after it. Since you're both Alexanders you can slip that past them and they won't notice but make sure you do it legally and with all the right papers. Get rid of all those bloody hangers-on. A single man doesn't need more than a dozen servants if he lives simply and they're all rogues who'd have the milk out your tea and come back for the sugar after. Your steward tells me you have a hundred of them out there on the farm, men, women, children – cleaning your shoes, powdering your hair, wiping your arse – as well as the other thing.'

'Don't burst a gusset, brother, I can afford them.'

'And for God's sake sort out your accounts with the Company. Stop ignoring them. I hear from London that Raffles is furious with you. They're trying to make him pay all your costs out of his own pocket.' A bat swooped out of the darkness, scooping up the cloud of smoky-flavoured mosquitoes dancing over their heads. 'Don't put the cart before the horse and kill the goose that lays the golden eggs. Sooner or later the chickens always come home to roost.'

***

'Look at it this way, Grimsby. Twilight of empire. We all have to make an effort. Us Brits are out, the locals are in. Get that through your head once and for all and everything will be a lot simpler. Everything east of Suez is going west.' Battersby grinned. The expression had come to him in the club the other night and he had used it on several occasions. Rather good he thought.

Outside, in the grounds of the governor's Istana, deer raised their heads nervously to sniff the breeze of a wind of change. Khaki troops in currant bun berets marched up and down, crashing their boots down on the cheap and guiltless tarmac. With the easing of the terrorist attacks up north in Malaya, there were suddenly a lot of them around again, driving up and down in trucks, getting under everyone's feet and the place, anyway, had never quite recovered from what the Japanese had done to it and still had the air of a Home Counties barracks. Not that troops were needed here. The terrifying figure in the front office kept all at bay – Aida Binti Nasir – a formidable Malay secretary with a beehive hairdo that seemed to buzz with real bees. When Arthur turned up, she had a great basket of shrivelled chillies on her desk and was slowly snipping them up with huge office scissors, clearly a chore left over from home, hands never idle.

Never let it be said that Arthur Grimsby had no manners. He smiled politely. 'I'm here to see the governor's PA. The name is Grimsby, Arthur Grimsby.'

Aida Binti Nasir curled her lip sceptically, cast a withering gaze at his infidel, uncircumcised crotch and snipped. 'You have an appointment? We are all very busy here. Mr. Battersby sees no one without an appointment.' Snip.

'Yes I see your busyness but I do have an appointment. By

telephone I made an appointment.' Said very quietly but firmly.

Aida paused like a kettle about to boil and scream with expelled steam, turned and looked sourly in her book, pointing with her scissors. 'It says here a Mr. Gimbley.' She turned back to her chillies. Snip. He was vaguely aware of a children's story where someone went around snipping off the thumbs of wayward children with huge shears but here the implied target was more than thumbs. God forbid that he should dare to openly correct her.

'I think that must be me. I have a name some people find difficult. Sometimes I am Mr. Gimbley or Grimy. On rare occasions, I have even been Grumbly.'

She glared and menaced with her scissors. 'What is this? You must decide what your own name is and stick to it. You are not a child. You cannot go about confusing people by using different names.'

'Well, I didn't actually ...'

She shook the basket of chillies in rustling reproof and a cloud of fiery dust rose up to which she was immune but acted on Arthur like teargas so that he fell back, coughing and sneezing. She reached angrily for the phone. 'There is a Mr. Grunty to see you, sir. Very well.' She hung up both grimly and grumbly. 'Go in. Now!' As he went through the door he saw her narrow her eyes and take aim again. Snip.

'Ah it's you. I wondered who the hell Grunty was.' Arthur wheezed in, sneezing into a handkerchief and groped across the room through running eyes for a chair. It was a clean hankie. Foresight. 'Sit down, Grimsby. I say that's a terrible cold you have.

For God's sake don't give it to me what with all we've got on our plate at the moment. Unlike you I can't allow *myself* the luxury of being ill. I'm terribly sensitive to such things. One sneeze near me and my mucus membrane turns into a mucus tarpaulin.' He shrank back as though from the touch of a leper.

Battersby was seated at his desk in shirtsleeves with those odd garters on the sleeves that only dynamic American newspaper editors are supposed to wear in films as they send the front page to press with a screaming headline that spins round before settling. He was busily trampling his signature over a stack of papers despite a clutter of abandoned accessories scattered across the surface – tie, cufflinks, penknife, reading glasses. He was a bustling sort of man with eager-beaver teeth and bat ears. The office exhibited sumptuary symbols in a manner that Hare's Dutch would have approved of – throw rugs, a hat stand, a vase of non-exuberant flowers, a telephone like Wayland's anvil, a swivel chair with leather pad. A ceiling fan and a desk fan batted the hot air back and forth between them as if wearily interrogating a terrorist suspect the way they did up north by slapping of cheeks from side to side. The desk fan swivelled. Battersby swivelled. Papers strained to escape into the breeze. His office was a wind tunnel.

'Why I sent for you … Look at it this way, Grimsby. Twilight of empire. We all have to make a special effort.' He sucked on his teeth. 'Us Brits are out, the locals are in. Get that through your head once and for all and everything will be a lot simpler. Everything east of Suez is going west.' He looked up, hoping for a titter, got none and continued, frowning. 'Whitehall will fix the final date for independence any day now, so we have to move the locals into positions of power and responsibility before we cut and run. Everything's being shifted forward, no time for dragging things out. Apart from anything else, it takes the wind out of the communists' sails if the wicked imperialists really are booking their tickets and going home. Anyway, the reason I called is we've decided you're next for the chop. So congratulations! The people here think they're the ones getting their freedom. They don't realise it's us old plough horses of empire, chafing under the heavy yoke of duty, that are being unharnessed and put out to grass – or perhaps to stud, eh?' He guffawed and winked horribly. 'Not me yet of course. The last legionnaire in the last fort, lowering the flag and all that. Have a word with the repatriation chaps to sort out the details, there's a good fellow, and best of luck to you. Apart from that, everything tickety-boo?'

Arthur swayed in this gale of news. No wait. That, surely, was the fan beating him about the face like a startled pigeon. He remembered a pigeon glimpsed tragically as a child in Trafalgar Square, hobbling on leprous feet, felt his own toes shrivel and legs go as he tried to rise and slumped back in the chair and the room went grey and began to spin about him in the blades of the fan. Of course, he had always known logically that, one day, something like this would happen, but this had caught him unawares, sideswiped him, come like Judgement Day but mentioned casually like a school's sports day in assembly. He had never had any interest in abstract politics, regarding such a concern as a worrying sign of dawning dementia. Questions echoed through his head like the booming voice of God. What would he do? Where would he go? How would he live? Most terrible question of all – the thunderous question of Faust but also of every petulant teenager – who was he now? An old man needs a confirmation of his own tortuously acquired identity and, suddenly, he realised, he was seen as an old man, looking backwards not forwards.

Battersby's droning voice emerged from the audible fog – Arthur suddenly recognised a Liverpool whine hiding in there somewhere – saying something about … 'Oh, sorry, by the way, to hear about your wife, Grimsby. I don't believe I ever actually said it.' Blood thundered in his ears as if after a damning medical prognosis. He looked up and saw the beaver teeth moving relentlessly as though chewing through a tough sapling. 'She's greatly missed down at the club. She was terribly popular, you know, a terrific sport.'

'Sport'? That was the polite word used for a girl who was easy and regarded sex as a sort of table-hopping whist drive. Surely Battersby could not be one of the … Eileen would not …

'I say, Grimsby, are you all right? You look a bit pale. Let me offer you a glass of water.' He poured from a dusty carafe. Don't get in a flap. Cheer up old man, it may never happen.'

Chapter Two

'Fiddlefaddle' was the light word Hare used to refer to the habits of his somewhat irregular domestic establishment and dismiss any serious concerns it might raise. Arthur thought that Alexander Hare must have quickly recognised that shipping it, lock, stock and barrel, from Java to South Africa had been a grave mistake. He had been given his marching orders by the Dutch of Java but there were nearly as many disapproving Dutch at the Cape as in the Indies and they were permanently disgruntled over the recent British takeover and equally eager to find examples of British degeneracy to make their own virtue shine forth. The farm, 12 miles from Capetown, had kept his 'family' out of town and out of mischief – it was important to keep them busy like Aida Binti Nasir – but it had been stupid to try to convert his domestic slaves into field hands, beating dusters into ploughshares. No one is more aware of relative rank than a slave or touchier about it. There were arguments – those received as royal gifts sneering at those who had been merely purchased in trade so that bargain basement buys felt themselves disrespected by the carriage trade of slavery. Moreover, Hare had sown the seeds of yet more discord by acquiring some black ladies – Arthur thought of them as Maria and Anna – to augment his collection and they were then treated as inferiors by the lighter-skinned Asians while some bleached, Chinese ladies who came onto the market at knockdown prices – vaginas allegedly strengthened by traditional footbinding – sneered, in turn, at everyone else, even disdaining Hare's own weathered and windbeaten copper complexion. He was intrigued by their tiny lotus feet, with the toes folded under to cover the sole so that they could scarcely hobble about the house – though it was said to be their haunting smell, never unbound and never washed – that reduced Chinese male aficionados to quivering lust.

There had come the sudden windfall of 83,000 Spanish dollars from the East India Company in consideration of his claims in Borneo – rasping parsimony replaced by a sudden gush of bounty. Hare had finally worn them down and wearied them into a settlement but the arbitrariness and unpredictability of the Company's decisions in Calcutta and London only made it seem even more like God and perhaps that is why Governor Lord Henry Somerset, one of the Company nobs, a man said to have a stronger claim to the English throne than the English king, held himself to be God's representative on earth at the Cape.

'It won't do, Hare.' Somerset was gaunt and adamantine, fashionably dressed as if sitting for a swagger portrait. He went through a lengthy and leisurely ritual of taking a gold snuffbox from his waistcoat pocket, tapping it pettishly, setting a pinch between thumb and forefinger and snorting it up in high-nosed derision. As a man not to be sniffed at, Hare barely resisted the temptation to pull out his even more ornate box and respond in kind, filigree curlicue for filigree curlicue. 'We have enough problems of our own, what with the Xhosa and the Dutch. Our own Malays are an insolent bunch, being troublemakers exiled here from Java by the Dutch. The treaty should have sent them packing back to Java but there you are. And your people have given them encouragement in their obstinacy through the rioting on your farm, smashing of windows and firing of crops. Thank God they all have each other to fight with and not just us. We have to set a certain example here and avoid both profligacy and effeminacy. I am convinced that you would easily find other locations more congenial to an oriental lifestyle such as your own. Our Dutch citizens are particularly and irritatingly engaged in the matter of domestic morality – not that they do not permit themselves any old thing under the starched tablecloth. Many have a powerful lack of imagination and, indeed, pride themselves upon it and cultivate it assiduously in their young and you will appreciate that letters have preceded you from their kinsmen in Java concerning the conduct of your own household there.'

'Letters? What letters, my lord? Who from and saying what exactly? Morality is not the same as conventionality, my lord, and conventionality is not a cloth cut to the same pattern in different climes.'

Somerset shrugged and waved a hand distractedly. 'I think that rather depends on one's station in life, don't you? What's sauce for the goose is gross impertinence for the gander, haha! Let me just observe that Madeira is said to be a most agreeable location at this season and you might do well to look into it.' The irritation of his aristocratic nostrils finally crystallised into a sneeze that he trumpeted away into a flourish of snowy-white silk handkerchief that was like a waved farewell.

This was the man, Hare reminded himself, who had added a huge ballroom to the gubernatorial mansion at public cost and been openly accused of buggery with the notorious army physician, Dr. James Barry. That Barry ultimately turned out to be a woman in male disguise did not in the least refute the charge. The English had always sent their sexually irregular abroad. For the merely incontinent, a Parisian exile sufficed. For gentlemen of unusual sensibility, the shores of the Mediterranean beckoned and the Levant offered an accepted tradition of pederasty but the greater the perceived perversity, the further you were required to travel south and east, so that you really had to wonder what they got up to in Australia. And Somerset was a man who had reason to fear moral panics. He had even botched a public hanging of Boers, converting what was intended as a demonstration of implacable British justice into one of his own high-strung incompetence. Recall, prosecution, fudge or disgrace were clearly just around the corner for Somerset. But then, if he were found guilty of all charges, he might still well end up snugly in Parliament through family connections. Hare suppressed his needling irritation.

'Quite so, my lord. But your lordship will no doubt appreciate the heinous effects that may come from lending credulity to unproved slanders that creep into the public mind via the back door.' He had the satisfaction of seeing his lordship's ears glow red as the stiletto slid between the ribs. 'Know then that the Cape is, for me, a mere provisioning station. The farm is to be sold. My people are already aboard my vessel and we await only a favourable opportunity to sail. I had intended to return to England but the current unclear state of the law there makes the reception of my household a matter of uncertainty.'

Fifty years back there had been that famous lawsuit about a slave called Somerset forcibly removed from England by his owner, though the legal decision against the owner had been fudged to avoid speaking out on slavery in general. Mentioning that would be delightful too – a punch to his lordship's tender nose – but going too far.

They were seated in one of the reception rooms with the big windows open to catch the cold wind coming up from the Southern Ocean as the last of the morning fog was burning off but Hare had put on his best bib and tucker for this interview and was still horribly hot. On the mantle, a great clock, its case all brass crust and bluster, ticked loudly. His father would have made a better one than that. The parquet flooring underfoot was a practical demonstration of the many tropical woods in which the Company dealt – quotation doubtless available on request. Hare knew them all and their prices, though the East India Company would up them as easily as Somerset his eyebrows if there was the slightest suggestion of a rise in demand. There was a nice piece of swirly amboina there under Somerset's left chair leg balanced by a slice of serviceable rosewood under his right.

But Hare was not being strictly honest. His 'family' were on shipboard primarily to prevent them running away, having been lured aboard with tales of being returned to Java – something now finally made impossible by the Dutch authorities – their protests hushed by lurid stories of the Xhosa cannibalism dealt out to runaway slaves. His soured relations with the Company made all other British possessions as a place of settlement ill-advised. His family had been declared free by the British authorities in Bengkulu yet made to swear to remain with him and not to seek employ elsewhere. The bewigged distinction had escaped them and they still believed themselves slaves.

Somerset tapped his foot impatiently on an embedded cut of yellow jackfruit tree. 'The vessel *Hippomenes* has been tied up in the harbour for many months, incurring diverse unpaid charges. It cannot long continue so without becoming unseaworthy and blocking the dock. It might easily be subject to seizure. Is it, in fact, your own vessel?'

Hare turned red as if himself subject to a seizure. He forced his expression back into a turd-eating smile. 'Partly so, my lord. The majority shareholding is in the name of my brother but it is a joint venture. All reasonable charges will naturally be paid in due course.'

'Then pray let me not delay your *prompt* departure any longer, Mr. Hare, and please ensure that you do not accidentally leave any baggage behind.'

Somerset pushed his chair back and rose on Makassar ebony and took an expensively shoe-shod step towards the door on fragrant sandalwood, indicating the meeting was over.

Hare smiled to himself, being aware that that sandalwood under the gubernatorial foot was blatant counterfeit, some cheap softwood dyed yellow to deceive the ignorant and gullible. But Somerset was a total fool who knew nothing of the ways of the East.

They were putting up new flats in Toa Payoh, poky, shoddy-looking affairs of steel wire and concrete, and there was bamboo scaffolding and construction everywhere as the old *kampung* houses were torn down and thrown in a great timber heap that was prodded to matchwood by some great crushing machine. Dust devils were skittering among the piles of dirt and sand, carried by a hot wind. Across the road, one creaky old survivor stuck out like a sore thumb, that of the guardian of the spring, an equally creaky old woman who swept it clean and looked after the offerings of bananas and joss sticks made by the faithful and the fearful. A handwritten sign clamped in a bamboo stem announced her resolve not to be moved. She looked like Bok's mother, a fragile woman whose curse would therefore carry a lot of weight.

Arthur parked the Morris under a shade tree and waited for the bus to arrive. A few minutes later it drew up with a shudder and the door slid back and out tumbled a mix of old ladies, sticky-fingered schoolboys and tired-looking men. Most thanked the driver as they passed to the door, gentle village ways lingering on in the faceless city. The flow was interrupted by a stiff-legged man on two sticks swivelling awkwardly down the steps, right and left, and at first it seemed that all the passengers had disembarked – and then she was there.

He ducked down below the level of the roof and watched Violet Loo as she crossed the road and trudged towards one of the old shophouses, its doorway framed by a display of tin shovels and red, plastic buckets. Perhaps the idea was that local children should treat the heaps of builder's sand as an improvised beach. Fronds of some vegetable stuck out of her bag as she made her way to the back of the shop to howled familial greetings. She paused to stroke an overfed cat that wriggled ecstatically under her touch. The hair at the back of her head was pasted to her skull with sweat and her feet looked heavy in their sensible office shoes as she clumped over the concrete into the dark interior.

At one moment, she turned back and looked over her shoulder and he crouched down, in terror of being spotted at his research. What would she think if she saw him? What would he say? What had come over him? Why the hell was he even here anyway?

* * *

Hare and the captain were on prickly terms at best. He was the brother of the John Ross who had been manager of his Mokolo sultanate and would now be winding up the new mess left behind on his African farm with its unharvested crops and broken windows and contracts. Perhaps, then, this Ross should be termed 'the lesser spotted Ross' to distinguish him from John. He was certainly a fellow Shetlander and bristling with all their usual resentments, real or imaginary. Brothers were the curse of the India trade. The lesser spotted Ross did not like being held up so long in port. He did not like having an owner aboard, giving him orders. He did not like being told, at the last minute, that their destination was not Java but Christmas Island.

'Why Christmas Island, for God's sake? You can't land

there. It's high cliffs all round, heavy surf, rocks. Arse-end of the universe and there's nothing of value there. No people. Only crabs. Nothing but a great heap of birdshit.'

Secure in his authority, Hare smirked in his face. 'Nothing at all on the island, you say? No inhabitants? Just shit?' Collett had written something about wherever you went in this world you would find Scotsmen and rats. 'Not even Scotsmen among the shit? Unusual that. If so, then you make it sound ideal for my purposes.' The world, he felt sure, had been unjustly cruel towards him and he could establish himself here with his people, set up his own little kingdom of birdshit and crabs, hold firm but benevolent sway over it, immune to nations and governments and their silly wars, finally be free to be and do whatever he wanted. He would remain totally safe from outside intrusion, like the rulers of Japan and China who suffered none to enter their domains and none who left to ever return. Compared to them, his own dream seemed really rather modest.

'It's nothing but a useless lump of rock. I won't risk my ship by attempting a landing.'

Hare glared. 'It is not *your* ship, Ross, but *mine*. You will do as I say, captain, even though I suppose that being a Shetlander makes you something of an expert on useless lumps of rock.' He turned on his heel and stalked away laughing, leaving Ross fuming on the expensive Javanese teak deck.

The ship skimmed over the corrugated waves, burying its nose in the foam, bounding like a hound glad to finally have a run off the leash after so many months' confinement. Flying fish preceded them, arcing in the sunlight, rainbows ricocheting off their bodies.

Hare's people knew nothing, of course, landlubbers all, since they still headed, as if for home, towards Java. For the first time in months, they would have been happy – had they not all been below retching and vomiting and praying to their various gods for a speedy and merciful death that would relieve their suffering.

***

Arthur stared at the stranger in the bathroom mirror with dispassionate puzzlement. Morning and late night brought their own form of terrible wisdom and self-knowledge. He had seen a portrait somewhere by Egon Schiele that celebrated the horror of human flesh and here it was revealed, stripped to the bone, in this horrible caricature. He was in his fifties, like Hare, but, unlike him, beyond all hope of creating new worlds, indeed, soon to be scrapped as irrelevant and outdated. His whole life was a huge heap of birdshit. With age, the curve of the mouth was naturally downwards not up, as in youth. That was to be expected. It was gravity was responsible, then, but what sort? Newton's implacable force working through time or pompous self-regard settling over his features? Just the weight of one's teeth or the weight of one's experience? Perhaps it was mere generalised fatigue. Having fun, even seeing fun in the outside world, demanded energy – like sending out radar. There was none of that youthful force pulsing in those eyes, no sparkle, no anticipation of pleasure or surprise to be had. They were blank like those of a dead fish in a museum case. They seemed rather to ask the world, 'What are you going to hit me with next?' Those eyes were not windows on the soul any more than Violet Loo's but just a place for the protective blink reflex to live and if they held any glint at all, it would be the start of a cataract.

Arthur's first reaction to what he was about to do was to shiver and then he was surprised to feel a sort of grim resolve settle in his neck and jaw as he reached for the razor, an old-fashioned, ivory-handled cutthroat that his father had left him. Somehow, it had survived the Japanese occupation and been just lying there on the shelf when he returned from Changi to take up where he had left off and slip back into his old self like an old cardigan. He flipped it open and set it in a line just above the Adam's apple, feeling the welcome, thin coldness of the eternal blade against the yielding, clammy skin. Take it on the jaw. Stiff upper lip. He paused one last time, looked into those blotted, joyless eyes, took a deep breath and raised his elbow for the first, firm and irrevocable stroke. In a few minutes the beard he had worn since Changi prison had swirled away down the sink in a grey, greasy soufflé, completely gone. He was a new man.

***

There was a hunched meanness about Christmas Island with no hint of tropical opulence. Sheer cliffs rose from the sea with spiny rocks scattered at their base like broken dentistry. No plants clung to them for none could survive the salt spray thrown up by the heavy Pacific rollers that swept in from thousands of miles of deep ocean to dash themselves against the island's walls with a frenzied death wish and a sound of artillery. In hollows beyond the boiling cliff face, crouched scabby coconut palms, their topmost leaves peering fearfully down at the ship below. Further inland, were hills with other trees trickling down their sides and the unmistakeable, silvery gleam of fresh water. They sailed along the coast in a weary, battering wind that yearned to drive them ashore and glimpsed the occasional spit of sand that only meant there was a hidden reef somewhere below the ship in the boiling water, just waiting to rip the bottom out of her with its jagged spikes, so they dared not venture closer in. Flights of seabirds wheeled and turned in the evening sky, their screeching audible in the pauses of the sea thunder. They were probably Christmas frigate birds but Hare would not have known that.

'This would be a terrible place to die,' said Ross, gripping the wheel, his words snatched away by the wind.

Hare turned and sneered. 'All places are terrible places to die but this would be a fine enough place to live in great economy. There's wood, coconuts, fish, birds' eggs and fresh water and it's a natural fortress. Any man installed here could withstand an army and set the whole world at defiance. Put off a little and wait out the night and we'll try again in the morning.'

Ross sighed. 'As you wish, Mr. Hare. But if the Javanese from up north didn't settle this place you can be sure it's not fit for human habitation. Those tough little buggers would build a house and thrive on the back of a turtle's shell.'

They sailed around the island, scanning for a landing place and found only a rudimentary cove with the hope of an easy climb to the top of the cliffs. At low tide, the breakers on the reef were visible. In one spot there were no breakers, suggesting a gap that might be navigable.

'Lower the longboat. We'll make a landing.'

'That's madness, Mr. Hare! In these seas, with those eddies inside the reef? Do you know what the tidal flow of water would be through a gap like that?'

'Give me just four of your best men.'

'I'll not.'

'Will you not, Mr Skeely Skipper? Well, benefactions speak louder than words.' Hare turned to the grinning crew, mainly Javanese, who were trying to work out what this argument was all about and shouted in Malay, 'A guinea for every man as rows me ashore in the longboat!'

They looked at each other and six leapt to the oars, repelling all boarders while Ross glared in impotence and the little boat was lowered and manned and cast adrift, bobbing like a cork on the fat, heaving swell, Hare manning the rudder and shouting quite unnecessary commands that the men simply ignored. They knew their business, drew clear, came about and lined themselves up and there came a pause as the men lay on their oars. Hare could be seen cursing and then digging in his pocket. Of course. They were asking to be paid before the attempt, knowing that if he drowned they would certainly not be paid after. Anyway, better to spread the gold about lest the weight of it drag him under. Then they were pulling hard, leaning into the oars, to pick up one of the heavy ocean rollers that lifted them like a feather and bore them with gathering speed towards the gap. They shot through, water towering on either side as high as a house and, just as it seemed that danger was past, the prow of the boat was gripped in a huge whirlpool that span them round like a top, flinging them violently over and engulfing the boat in water.

A huge mass of ocean water crashed down on their heads. Hare found himself in seething currents, struggling vainly towards the surface from a black and bottomless pit, coughing and spluttering, fighting for his life in a suddenly hushed and gloomy underwater tomb of shadows. It seemed like an eternity and he was about to embrace the inevitability of death when he was grabbed by two Malays, swimming like fish, who bore him up so he burst back into a world of light and sound as they dragged him away from the reef into calm and shallow water. The others were laughing and shouting, had already righted the boat and clearly regarded the near-lethal experience as great sport as they gathered up the oars. He grabbed the side of the boat, shaking and shuddering, desperately cold despite the heat of the sun, stammering his thanks. He looked at the terrifying passage they had come through and fear gripped him anew at the thought of returning through that.

'How the hell will we ever get out again?' he gibbered. This would never do. In the monsoon season, they could be cut off for months. The women and stores would never manage the landing.

The Malays laughed and sprawled back in a tangle of easy, relaxed limbs. 'This is nothing, *tuan*. We will wait for the tide to turn again and, when the wind comes round in the afternoon, it will be easy to go back. We are lucky the sea was so peaceful today. Sometimes it is rough.'

In the evening, as they hauled the sodden parcel that was Hare back over the ship's rail, gasping and shaking, Ross was there gloating.

'You're not the first sailor that a healthy draught of seawater has brought round to my way of thinking, Mr. Hare.'

The next day, he offered the captain, smilingly, a tankard of hot rum toddy in reconciliation. Of course, he pissed in it first.

***

'Ayoooh!!' The cup of tea slipped from Violet Loo's small hands, hit the floor and smashed, flinging tea and custard creams to the four winds. In the civil service, the periods of the day were ruthlessly marked out in cups of tea and hierarchy was inscribed in the quality of the biscuits. She stared in horror at Arthur, the floor, at her dress, at the disruption of time itself. She pointed at him, then began to laugh, rocking back on her heels and raising both hands to cover her mouth.

'Dr. Grimsby! What happen? Where your beard? I don't recognise you when I come in. I think is ghost. You have accident? Hurt your face maybe?'

He looked up from his Hare notes and ran an exploratory hand over his smooth, boyish chin and grinned nervously. His whole face felt lighter, cooler, daringly naked and raw, exposed and self-aware, like a man when he steps out of the changing room in his swimming trunks and suddenly becomes scarily aware of his bulging or shrivelling manhood and the unwonted currents of air in which it moves.

It was odd that she wrote perfect English but spoke a form of Singlish with no endings and in an eternal present tense. An anthropologist would build a theory of the universe out of that. 'The Singapore Chinese live in the present with no sense of their past or care for tomorrow, this makes them the people of the future.'

'Make you look younger.'

He blushed. 'It was time.' Looking down at the mess on the floor, he noticed her shoes. Perhaps it *was* time. They were no longer the clumpy Bata clogs left over from her schooldays that she usually wore. These were dainty, pink pumps not high heels certainly but slim and elegant though now stained with tea. 'Time for a change. I'm sorry, I should have warned you but, frankly, I didn't think anyone would notice. Now your new shoes are ruined.'

She looked down. 'Ha! You notice my new shoes? You like?' She pivoted and twirled in parody of a debutante. There was a note of delight in her voice – mostly surprise – but delight was definitely there as a grace note. Then, she reverted to herself and rubbed the tips of the toes down the back of her legs as schoolchildren are wont to do in a gesture that he found charming. 'Is nothing. Later I wash.'

Arthur went down, rather gallantly as he thought, on his knees like a proposing swain. 'Here let me help you clean up this mess. All my fault I'm sure.' He began gingerly to pick up broken china, stacking one piece on top of another with archaeological care and holding them out like a present. There was a time when Chinese set an empty pot on the front roof of a house where there was a marriageable girl to encourage the attentions of suitors. The groom would triumphantly smash it on the wedding night.

Probably Freud had put an end to such obvious symbolism even in Asia. After all, interpretation should make you strain a little if it was to do its unconscious job at all. Arthur stretched out his hands further reaching with the offering.

Violet Loo started back, horror-stricken and horribly affronted, eyes shocked wide-open, as if he had crudely reached out and grabbed her backside. 'Me clean up? Kennot-lah!' She stalked haughtily away through macerated biscuit rubble. 'Hah! Not *my* job to clean up. I send for cleaner.'

***

The Cocos-Keeling Islands were one of Nature's more delightful anomalies, some 27 low, coral islands split between two atolls, scattered halfway between Australia and Ceylon, territorial dandruff of the larger continents and now claimed by Hare. At the end of the 19th century, they would assume new prominence as the one spot on the map where all the undersea communication cables of the British Empire came together. Presently, they were uninhabited, unflagged, little dots of nowhere on a world map of jostling, proprietorial rights, a picture postcard waiting for the invention of the camera as a curious place where crabs ate coconuts, rats nested in the trees and shells of the mammoth tridacna mollusc might trap and eat incautious human divers. But settlers would not starve for there were birds and their eggs, cruising turtles, and the lagoons teemed with fish, queuing up to be caught.

Some men found nations out of an inflated sense of their

own importance or to seize free goods for themselves or justify the grabbing of the wealth of others. In Hare's time, nationalist motives of planting the flag loomed large and were conventionally held to be nobly creditable. But all Hare wanted – in anticipation of Greta Garbo – was to be alone – alone with his people that is – and hold himself aloof. And the Cocos-Keeling Islands, a mere 500 miles from Christmas Island, would do nicely. There were no resources to excite the cupidity of others – not even birdshit – no dangerous beasts, a mild climate with adequate rainfall and lots and lots of coconut palms – that ultimate symbol of tropical paradise in whose shade he intended to re-enact the myths of apple-bearing Eden by disporting himself with his ladies in the midst of redemptive Nature.

But, as in Eden, there is the problem of brothers. Hare's captain is the lesser spotted Ross. The greater spotted Ross, John Ross, known grandly in a later work as Ross Primus, would maintain he had already explored Cocos-Keeling with the aim of establishing his own settlement there and even planted experimental crops in anticipation of his return. But does pushing a banana into the soil establish *droit de seigneur*? And who exactly drew Hare's attention to the spot? Was it the lesser Ross himself, off guard and prattling in an incautious moment at the Cape? If he did so, was it as a treacherous brother finally gaining revenge for some festering fraternal slight of childhood? Or was it as a frustrated sea captain who just wanted Hare off his ship at any cost? Whoever takes the blame or the credit and whatever his motives, Hare landed there in June 1826 and declared Cocos his new home.

He disembarked with stores and followers and the ship sailed away. Exactly how many stood on that beach and watched it go under the terrifying emptiness of the sky, we do not know. Later estimates speak of 36 males, 25 females and 37 children but by then there had been numerous additions and losses. What the exact personal relationships were amongst that tiny knot of people and what they felt as the vessel dipped below the horizon and the tips of its masts finally disappeared, can only be a matter of speculation for they have no voices in the literature. They had been led to believe they were headed back to Java, home for most and now they were effectively marooned on a world so small you could look clean through it and out the other side as if they were jungle plants that suddenly realised they were trapped in a window box. What were they like? We always imagine that the oppressed bear a certain moral superiority – restoring balance to the world – and that the wronged should be gentle, stoical beings but there is every reason on earth, having suffered so much at the hands of a cruel and hostile reality, that they should be absolute swine.

Chapter Three

As a collector himself, Arthur realised that all collections are based on the same two conflicting principles – completeness and uniqueness. Raffles had collected fine objects to show off the wealth and beauty of the Indies and carried them back to a sceptical London but when sociological diversity was to be exemplified, he commissioned little, painted, wooden carvings of 'social types' that stood on neat, wooden plinths like china ornaments for the mantelpiece. Hare considered this a poltroon approach and had gone one further and built a collection of genuine human specimens and his harem had as much geographical spread as possible – Java, Sumatra, New Guinea, Africa, China, India but one man could never hope to attain full coverage of the Orient and celebrate the splendour of its infinite human variety. How had Hare become such an avid collector in the first place? There were no clues in the documentation. Perhaps he found himself attracted by different features in many different women yet despaired of finding perfection in any single individual, so that his collection was a sort of jigsaw composite person. Or perhaps it was the equivalent of the *rijsttafel*, invented by the Dutch, who – when faced with the overwhelming variety of traditional Asian food – created a meal that consisted of dozens of little dishes, all different, and so removed the need for a definitive choice that would have reduced it to a proper meal of meat and two veg.

Whatever the reason, Hare was like a man gazing into an ethnic kaleidoscope and fascinated by the differences of human forms, the variability of skin colour – porcelain to chocolate, the texture of hair – straight, kinky, wavy – the shape of noses – hooked, flattened, pert and eyes, oh how he loved eyes – round, almond-shaped, slit – that flashed darkly but differently beneath lashes like the wings of every kind of butterfly. In the East, it was of course true that all eyes were brown, lacking the sheer colour variety of Europe, but they went far beyond the leached tea and hazel shades of English brown, favouring the deep and beguiling hues of jet and polished mahogany. Then there was the added possibility of deliberate deformation and enhancement – skulls shaped by binding, tattoos, piercings, filed teeth, lips spread and plugged, tongues slit and pierced – enhancing and extending the glorious diversity of Nature or of God. There had once been girl with a harelip back in the same street in Clerkenwell whom he had studied on his way to school, a dwarf in Malacca whose disproportions had fascinated him through many a hot afternoon. And, in sex, even cries of pleasure and pain, gasps and groans, different bodily positions, varied from place to place on the map. At what point did humanity merge and become one? Boundaries remained to be finally fixed. It had only recently been established that, among some races, women could not spontaneously conceive through excessive exposure to the tropical sun. Sex was multivarious and had obsessed many great minds. Captain

Cook had been driven to explore the myths of Hottentot sexual difference though his conclusions had been fed swiftly to the flames by his timorous wife and Hare was even intrigued by tales of Australian Aborigines who carefully dyed the soles of their feet so that when they fell over blind drunk they remained attractive to the ladies.

Yet Arthur suspected that Hare's performance of the sexual act with his collection – though deemed by him good in itself like the taste of ripe fruit – was to be seen primarily as a deed of registration, more to do with incorporating them fully into the whole, as a bibliophile might dip his brush in the glue pot and paste his bookplate into a new volume before he placed it on the shelf under its proper heading and stood proudly back to admire its calfskin binding, its gilt edging and its embossed spine. Thereafter, he might be content merely to display and handle and admire. Such acts absorbed Hare into Asia and Africa and them into him. His was the world's first ethnographic seraglio and a fully working collection. What did the girls make of all this? It turned them into objects and museum objects traditionally have no voices of their own – but even dead people tell tales and Arthur was anxious that the girls should speak if only in his imagination.

The mistress of Hare's household, Siti, was not pleased. She was a handsome, dark-skinned woman with good bones but when men call a woman 'handsome' it means she has other attributes than sexiness that have effectively neutered her. With growing rotundity, she had long since ceased to be one of Hare's paramours and moved on to higher, curatorial functions, her solidity being read as reliability, but she felt that the thirteen girls in her hands were insufficiently under her thumb. The proud mark of her office, Hare's silver badge of the East India Company slung around *her* neck since they had got rid of the Malacca wife, was treated with scant regard by her charges. She must discipline the girls, somehow rule them but not damage them too much. Siti was skilled in the ways of pleasing a man and taught them to her charges as recruits learn basic drill and was expert in treating women's problems or in easing away an unwanted pregnancy with bitter herbs and pressing fingers. *Tuan* Hare disliked babies and had any woman with one sent away as disturbing of his peace. And she had learned a lot about dealing with insubordination and conflict, jealousy and spite and running a group of women under the blanket of sisterhood. Often, she could use their own beliefs against them. The Borneo girls lived in terror of being swiped with a broom, the touch of whose bristles was doom-laden, while the Javanese feared the pig bristles she was known to preserve in a little box and that could slip so easily into their rice and the Malaccans trembled at the thought of the dust from the tomb of infidel priest Ignatius Loyola that might appear, at any moment, beneath their sleeping mats.

But the two African girls, Maria and Anna, seemed in awe of nothing and were a problem – it was hard to tell them apart – after all, all black faces looked the same to her. Then, they were physically intimidating – small but muscular and stronger than Hare even – with loud, scary voices and big, pink-palmed, black hands that frightened the other girls. How could he sleep with them? They were so black and ugly. It was an insult to the other girls who took such pains to be pale, shading their skins and rubbing in bleaching ointments for hours every day to preserve their beauty. They talked to each other in a strange, clicking language like woodpeckers and spoke to Hare in easy English to his face or a kind of pidgin Dutch he found hard to follow. They had been the ones who started all the trouble at the Cape and stirred up the men to riot with their insidious needling. They had been bought cheaply, two for one, because the Arab traders who first brought them down from the north thought them too heavy in the rump for the Western taste and they had a previous history of running away to join the country maroons, being only recaptured at great expense. They remained unrepentant. Worse still, they were now Christians which encouraged arrogance, thinking they had immortal souls and were therefore every bit as good as their master.

The last resort was violence and Siti had not hesitated to try to slap Maria into obedience. To her astonishment, the girl had simply pulled back her arm and let fly an answering slap that nearly knocked her teeth out of her head so that she wore the mark of that great shovel-like hand on her cheek for days and the other girls sniggered at it behind her back. That had never happened before, since Siti was skilled in coaxing or breaking shy and unwilling girls, though most simply accepted their fate within the seraglio as the way the world was. It was a world where girls, whether slaves or free, grew up to be sold off to older men who used them as they pleased whether as wives, casual mistresses or concubines. The most they could hope for was one who was a little kind or just rich and indifferent or old and impotent and the satisfactions of matrimony lay mostly in the hope of a child that could give and receive real love or the hushed Sapphic delights of the harem. But, on their first night, these two had just gone in fearlessly to Hare and, in the morning, they simply strode out, brazenly naked, clicking at each other, laughing and contemptuous in a surge of huge breasts, slick with sweat and sexual fluids, while Hare had staggered to the bedroom door in his nightshirt, red-faced and haggard.

Siti was appalled. Asian polygamy did not preclude a certain straight-lacedness about the house. But curiosity triumphed over prudery in the short term. She looked and was astonished at the sheer size of their naked buttocks as they passed, deprived of any hint of covering, and then they turned again and she screamed out loud, clasping her hands to her mouth and mumbling a Muslim prayer in sheer terror. The outer parts of these she-devil vaginas had been stretched like Dayak ears and hung down boldly smacking their lips at her and their bellies were criss-crossed with raised scars as though they had been raked by tigers.

'Allah!' she screeched and moved her hands to clap them over her eyes.

The girls laughed again and strolled off insolently to bathe together. She was not to know that their pleasure came not from physical fulfilment but from a common purpose. They had decided to kill Alexander Hare and they would kill him by turning the tables, use his own greed and sexual pride against him, pursue him for endless gratification, day and night, milk him like a Zulu cow, harass him, ridicule his flagging masculinity, wear him down, wear him out, invade his sense of privacy and self until he could bear it no longer.

'To oppose him is not the way. It will only make him angry and hard to live with. Men like to see themselves as bold hunters. They like to think that sex is something that men do to women but their pride is easily turned against them so that they become as gelded farmyard beasts. It is the story of the tortoise and the elephant,' said Maria. Anna raised her eyebrows. 'You do not know it?

Once upon a time there was a king who tried to capture a great elephant that lived in the bush. He sent his best warriors. Most did not come back as the elephant knocked them down with its huge trunk and crushed them to death under its feet. Those that did return, were broken men.

So the tiny tortoise said, "I will do it but in return you must give me half your kingdom." Everyone laughed at him. "How can a little thing like you defeat a great elephant when great warriors have failed?"

The tortoise just smiled. "We shall see what we shall see." Then the tortoise, who was a clever creature, went off and dug a big hole in the path to the palace and covered it with sticks and leaves.

He went to the elephant's house and called to him. "Oh, elephant," he cried. "Great lord. Men have decided to recognise your greatness and make you their king. They have asked me to bring you to the palace for your coronation."

The elephant was suspicious. "I do not believe you. Are not these the same people who have sent their warriors so many times to capture me and make me their slave?" he asked.

"That is why they see now that you are greater than any of

them. Come now in your magnificence and take your throne. Moreover, how could I who am so small and weak pose any danger to one as powerful as you?"

"Very well," said the elephant. "But you must walk before me and if there is any sign of treachery, I will kill you with my huge tusks. Look at how big and strong I am and how thick and long is my trunk."

"Very well. We shall see what we shall see."

And so they set off through the jungle and, when the people saw the tortoise just leading the elephant, they all cheered so that the elephant thought they must be rejoicing at his coronation and truly believed that was about to happen so that he felt more easy in his mind. When they reached the pit, the tortoise who was very weak and very light passed over easily but the elephant who was so strong and whose trunk was so heavy crashed through and was trapped. So the king's men came and took him easily and imprisoned him in chains and the tortoise became rich and powerful.'

Anna frowned. 'What does the story mean?' She had always been a dull girl and was soaping herself with equally dull soap that refused to lather. 'What has it to do with our plan?'

Maria sighed. 'Hare is the elephant. We are the tortoise that will slowly destroy him and we will make the other girls, those bleating sheep, help us too.

'How will we do that?'

Maria snapped her fingers and rubbed coconut oil over her shoulders and breasts. 'We will tell them we are witches and, that if they don't do as we say, we will kill them all, like that.' She snapped them again but, because of the oil, there was no click.

Anna gasped as she ladled cold water over her chest. 'Well. We shall see what we shall see. But there is one more thing I do not understand.'

'Yes?'

'What is an elephant?'

***

And then John Ross arrived in the *Borneo* to find a big, fat drongo cuckoo or rather a hare squatting comfortably in his nest. He saw himself as being like Moses, leading his people out into the Promised Land but, instead of a tribe of Israelites, brought only a brittle, shrewish wife, a God-fearing mother-in-law, pale, thumbsucking and snot-nosed children and a few brave, Bible-fed colonists who doubled up as crewmen. The dead hand of the Wee Free church lay heavy upon them, unable to get over the fact that humans were incarnated in flesh and not pure spirit. The only harbour entrance was now occupied by his employer and Ross was furious, of course, but there was a habitual deference established and he realised he would have to manage his resentments or be immediately ruined.

The whole basis of his intended business was the House of Hare. European traders arrived in the East seeking pepper, spice and other exotic cargoes and were forced to wait expensively tied up in dock, muttering against demurrage costs, seeing their crew running off, while cargoes were collected out in the backlands. Prices fluctuated wildly according to the season and the demand.

The unexpected arrival of another vessel could send them through the roof. Ross's plan was to establish the Cocos as an entrepôt port where crops could be stored for prompt shipment all year round, having been bought in when prices were at their lowest and so achieving the impossible – actually saving buyers money by inserting a middle man. But in this, the Hare brothers were essential both as agents and shippers. That Ross arrived in the *Borneo*, the ship he had built for Hare in Mokolo, hammered home his hard dependence. He avoided confrontation through gritted teeth, unloaded the *Borneo* on the beach and set off to complete the voyage to Sumatra and Java before coming back to finally settle himself. Arthur imagined that Ross's wife, a woman of strong, godly opinions and good lungs – who allegedly once saved him single-handed from a London Press Gang – would have unloaded on him since, like her mother, she cultivated that island virtue of 'frank speaking' that the rest of the world knows as sheer rudeness.

***

Arthur wondered what Hare felt for these ladies of his seraglio. To seek to make Hare express feelings that he may never have been able to express himself in any of his languages was a strange form of ventriloquism but truth and fiction differed in that the latter had to make sense while the former didn't. The fact that they were sexually accessible did not preclude other charms. Did he love any of them and, if so, with what sort of love? Love and lust are supposed to be quite separate things – love giving, lust taking – but the border between them is a fluid one, i.e. expressed in fluids that shift with the tide and intermingle their essences. Even with the same person, that mix is quite different at midnight and six in the morning. We naïvely assume that a slave-holder's sense of possession is something that overrides all other emotions but why should it? Did it necessarily preclude love? The extreme actions of Hare's later days were all interpreted through the eyes of Ross, a narrow-minded God-squadder, as deliberate evil, gleeful malevolence, and that assessment was accepted by later writers as simple fact. So Hare was unjustly accused of slave-trading, gun-running, even incest and murder but his deeds could as much be the deeds of a man driven to the edge of reason by the terror of desertion and loneliness as much as by outraged ownership. And, of course, possession might have been a two-way thing. The girls would feel jealousy if he showed preference to one of them over another so that it was as if *they* possessed *him*. Facts are often flexible yet moral judgements are easy when made on principal but only accurate when made according to circumstances.

The ultimate power would lie in violence, of course, and there was no shortage of appalling acts recorded by the Dutch against the slave population of the Indies. Yet, they mingled with stories of love and affection, marital and paternal, that show the complex vortices of the human heart. Arthur wondered whether the occasionally documented prosecutions of slave masters for cruelty were the sign of a generalised culture of physical and sexual violence, as he suspected, or the mark that such behaviour would not be tolerated. Which was the exception, the brutality or the prosecution and how far would Hare have been prepared to go?

Despite her protests to the contrary, Arthur had never felt it was the violation of his proprietorial rights that upset him when Eileen wandered from the straight and narrow. Love was not a zero-sum game where another's gain was his loss. It was rather that her appalling choices – men like Macclehose or others, military morons in yellowing Aertex vests – reflected so badly on him. It was like losing a beauty contest to a whole series of warthogs.

And Hare was not just a slave-master. He was above all a collector and Arthur knew that collectors may be insanely enamoured of their pieces, obsessed by them and the urge to preserve them, which is why they so often, paradoxically, give them away to enduring institutions. Possession may not negate tenderness. In his will of 1816/18, Hare bequeathed interest and profits from his capital of some £50,000 to 'all my Girls, slaves and their children born in my family' so that they could live out their lives together on some country estate and enjoy 'the sort of maintenance they have been accustomed to' but they should be spared excessive contact with any who might corrupt and debauch them and individuals should only be sold off as a very last resort. Paternalistic certainly, but not uncaring and – Arthur thought – much like the concerns of those dedicated donors of fragile and valuable objects to his museum who wanted their collections saved from the rapacious cut and thrust of the commercial sphere and eternally housed together. When drawn from distant parts, such collections were not to be seen as hostages held against their will but as refugees offered a safe haven and that's how Hare, the collector, might well have seen his women.

* * *

The Asian girls were gathered round an ornate board, carved like a dragon's head at one end, tail obligingly at the other, but with two rows of seven cups set along the spine. They had lugged it into the big hut that faced the open sea to catch any breeze of passage and were relaxed, barefoot and with just a sarong knotted over their breasts. Hare's assistant, Ogilvie, was padding about with his sharp little nose poking into everything, otherwise they would have worn even less. Two girls faced each other, their eyes wide with excitement, lost in the game. The others surrounded them in a hot, little huddle, waving their hands, shouting advice. The younger one scooped up a handful of tamarind seeds from one of the holes and began swiftly counting them out around the board, clockwise, one seed in each hole, grabbed more seeds from the last hole and set off again to mounting excitement, hands moving round the board and slowing to a conclusion. As she played out the last one and held up her hands to show they were empty, there came a scream of delight and laughter and the girls clapped their hands in pure glee and danced on the spot.

'*Congkak*,' Ayu of the bottomless eyes explained to Maria, pointing. Being from Bengkulu, she spoke a little English. 'We call it *congkak*.' She was in awe of the African girls and followed them around, acting as their mouthpiece.

'No,' shouted another in hot contradiction. 'In Java, *dakon*.'

'We say *dara-dara*.'

'*Galacang* in Sulawesi.'

'No, *meuta* or *sai*.'

Maria sniffed. 'Well, we call it *morabaraba* but our version comes with more holes and is more complicated.'

'Show us.'

Maria squatted down and began to scoop little depressions in the earth with bare hands until she had four neat rows in all. The girls watched, smirking at this rustic approach. 'More seeds. We need more seeds.'

They were brought and she divided them up and Anna came and sat, grinning wickedly across from her, hands dangling loosely in her lap. 'Now watch.'

It was a game of fiendish speed and complexity, the girls' hands flashing back and forth across the board, almost invisibly, as in some frenzied dance. They turned, counted scooped. New sub-rules were called into play, sub-sub-rules, the game transformed before their eyes, some holes now ignored or opponent's holes looted when the player's own was empty, fortunes rose and fell with incredible rapidity. The girls watched open-mouthed as the seeds flew. Ayu gobbled at the other girls and turned.

'Teach us.'

Maria paused and reflected. 'We will teach you. But we must play for something. To play for nothing is to play with empty hands.'

'We have no money. What may we play for?'

Maria smiled at Anna. 'I can think of something.' She leaned and whispered in the Bengkulu girl's ear and watched as her cheeks grew red and her eyes incredulous, finally collapsing in shocked giggles and writing away into the corner with her hands over her face.

* * *

Wherein lay the fascination of Violet Loo? Her very name denied the possibility of a glamorous and exotic East, the *houri* fragrances of the harem chased away in the associations of a nose-tingling waft of Harpic lavatory cleanser. No poet would ever write, 'I love you, Violet Loo, with a love so rare and true.' No, it would simply never do. He studied her as she bustled about the office in a cheap frock of loud colours. Birdwatching had taught him how to observe without seeming to, how to spend hours of patient waiting with most functions switched off. As long as you did not rest your eyes directly on them, birds would often ignore you and just go about their business untroubled. Yet, somehow, these eyes were no longer purely his. They were also somehow the eyes of Alexander Hare. She was not beautiful, he decided – her body was not curvaceous or steatopygous – though her features could be described as perfectly regular. Indeed, it was the lack of just those minute imperfections that make love rewrite the notion of beauty in our minds that made her fall short of beautiful – the slight disparity in size of an eye, the lopsidedness of a beloved smile, the lock of hair that resisted discipline. She had a sort of mass-produced, industrial prettiness, like a doll. That was it! She was doll-like, ceramic, to be broken like a Chinese pot on the roof. A china doll. She was an undangerous cartoon of the East and the Hare-like thought made Arthur want to twirl his moustache and slap his knee.

It occurred to Arthur that he had never heard Violet Loo express a single profound thought and the Singlish she used robbed her speech of any chance of saying anything beyond the superficial. After all, that's what creoles were designed for, to communicate but impoverish like headlines or poster slogans, to limit and confine thought to basic, material functions – like communist theory – kill the bosses and get more rice. Perhaps that was why communism went down so well in Singapore and Malaya. The British claimed they were winning the war against the terrorists with their secure New Villages that cut them off from supplies but Arthur suspected you couldn't contain ideas with barbed wire fences, especially ideas so simple that they were like ghosts.

He used the thought to suppress a beckoning daydream of Violet. She surely was unworthy of such strong passion, for where were the extraordinary qualities that could possibly justify it? Then he recalled in shame the words of some too-clever Frenchman, 'Men don't spit just with their mouths' and blushed with shame.

***

The boys sat cross-legged in the sand in a neat row, bright-eyed and alert, hair still wet from an afternoon spent riding the great turtles out in the lagoon. For them, island time was still stretched by the empty anticipations of childhood that kept boredom at bay. They had arranged themselves in descending order of height and age, running from about eighteen to eight, a classification cross-cut by that of skin pigmentation from purest Chinese porcelain to darkest Papuan ebony, forming a most satisfactory subcollection in Hare's view. It was odd that in their mating habits, most humans preferred to sleep with their own, like birds of a feather, and just paddle in a rockpool as opposed to swimming in the wide ocean. All the better, then, for those who celebrated variation, like Hare himself, as it prevented the degeneration of difference into a common and uninteresting ethnic sludge. For formal occasions, the boys had identical sarongs that further toyed with the notion of unity within diversity but today they were in tucked-up old cloths, bleached and thin with wear and ragged at the hem. They clutched the crumpled instruments they had been given tightly on their knees and giggled amongst themselves. As with all youth orchestras, even the most humdrum percussion was always more accomplished than brass, since mastery of rhythm came more readily than command of pitch and Indies boys anyway had the pulse of gamelan orchestras pounding in their blood. Oddly, the smallest lad played a huge, growling tuba whose weight he barely supported and whose coils seemed like a giant boa constrictor in the act of swallowing him up, while the tallest and huskiest was made master of the squeaky fife. A Balinese lad had seized the bugle and made it his own, cross-cutting the music with wild squeals anticipating jazz. The Chinese lads had been entrusted with the snare drums on the grounds that anything involving two sticks would sit more easily with them and the Papuans delighted in being sounding brass and tinkling cymbals but insisted they could not play unless they were allowed to stamp their feet rhythmically on the spot.

In his youth in distant London, Hare had enjoyed a rudimentary musical education and music remained for him, like sex, sheer delight conjured out of thin air. The digital dexterity of his pupils could not be questioned if the size of the holes dug under his storehouse wall by young thieves was to be believed. They were a light-fingered bunch, all right. Yet somehow these elements had formed the basis of a strangely dissonant harmony and they had rapidly progressed from random parpings and pipings to a rich and haunting sonorous sauce that could be poured over almost any melody. And they practised relentlessly. Anyone walking between the huts of the workers' *kampung* would have been astonished at some of the exuberant toots and farts they would hear at all hours of the day and night. Initially, they had been taken for the cries of threatening demons and spread hushed disquiet through the native huts, only dispelled by a staged first public performance by the band. Sometimes, Hare would send them out to play upwind of the Ross household on Sundays, at the churching hour, knowing Mrs. Dymoke held all music, as a source of human pleasure, to be the mocking laughter of the devil. He would dearly love to have included a set of sneering bagpipes, which would have irritated the Rosses immensely, but knew the boys would be terrified of them.

'Right, lads! Let's try "Heart of Oak" again. This time put your livers into it.' He raised his arms to lead them in.

They grinned and whispered. "*Hardsofock*" was a great favourite with them, especially the chorus '*Setedi boi setedi!*' that they would shout out as loudly as their instruments would allow, with big smiles on their faces.

They struck up with verve, straining to compete with the humbling vastness of the sky and ocean. Then, as they were just getting into it, one of the girls appeared, hipswivelling over the sand, with a dish piled high with cakes of coconut and palm sugar and set it down as their promised reward. It was a mistake. The practice swiftly became a race to the finishing line with the piccolo charging ahead of the tuba and the bugle screaming defiance to all in the rush to get to the cakes. On the last note, there was no holding them any longer. They dropped their instruments and flung themselves forward and fell in a great shameless heap, grabbing and chewing, stuffing the unaccustomed treats in their mouths and Hare dropped his arms, turned and walked away laughing.

Chapter Four

Maria and Anna knelt with bowed heads and clasped hands through the long hellfire prayer bellowed out by John Ross. Occasionally they stole sideways glances and fought not to giggle. They were neatly dressed in the long, white bombazine tents that Mrs. Dymoke, Ross's mother-in-law, had given them to protect their Christian modesty in the face of the shameless pagan girls of Hare's household. A major concern had been the fashioning of dowdy bonnets that would prevent the male caresses of the sun while still avoiding any suggestion of female vanity. After the service, they would take tea and practise their sewing. Their salvation was a work of Christian charity that she had carried forward in the teeth of initial opposition from both her son-in-law and Hare. The former had been mollified when he realised that it was an excellent way of learning what was going on in that godless institution of the House of Hare, the latter when he was convinced they were spying for him on the Rosses.

'Mr. Hare speaks so ill of dear Mr. Ross and denies he was the first to plan a settlement on the Cocos Islands so that he only remains here on Mr. Hare's sufferance. He says that all the coconut trees belong to him as first settler and that poor Mr. Ross has no right to harvest them as he is doing and he will put a stop to his dealing in their oil. He sets his own followers to press oil but that is merely to distract them. At night he secretly pours away what they have made as an excuse for rebuking them and working them even harder.'

'Mr. Hare says that your kind of Christianity is the invention of the devil and urges us not to come to your services any more at the risk of our immortal souls. Please do not let him prevent us, dear Mrs. Dymoke! We do not wish to burn in Hell for all eternity as you say we should.'

'Mr. Hare tries to force us into his bedchamber for purposes which we do not understand, which we have thus far resisted. We are simple country girls, confused in our innocence. When he lays hands on us we have no resource but to kneel together in prayer to our Lord and clasp our Bibles to our chests so that shame overcomes even him. But who knows how long that may last? He says, "Bugger the Bible". We do not know what that means.'

Mrs. Dymoke rounded on John Ross, ears aflame. 'Hare's house is a pit of immorality and a nest of vipers. Children of Sodom! Sinful prodigality with untold money spent to paint the faces of whores of Babylon while we are left to labour here in thrift and want. If you were a real man you would chase them out.' Ross's wife nodded grim assent. What he got from the one during the day, he would get from the other at night.

Arthur thought about that. Wait. It seemed more likely that, as men, Ross and his like would be sniffing around Hare's place themselves after windfalls of forbidden fruit. After all, there was a desperate shortage of women on the Cocos and, for the women, there was certainly more than just Hare on offer. The principal problem of Hare's Garden of Eden was that it was awash with other Adams and their writhing serpents. Surely, there would have been endless night time raids and escapades, trysts and whispered messages passed via the children. Young blood would have called out to young blood in a language spoken by all.

**

It was a peaceful day where Nature spoke with a lowered voice and in the rhythms of poetry. A cool breeze barely ruffled the waves and the roar of the surf out on the reef was lulled to a gentle murmur that was almost the contented purring of a great cat. Hare sat on a great ironwood throne beneath the swaying palms in the sort of silk pyjamas favoured by the Portuguese of Timor. A multi-hued, grandiloquent turban adorned his head as became a benevolent patriarch or a character from a Gilbert and Sullivan opera. He half-dozed in the warm air. After all, a gentleman's life should consist of alternate periods of indulgence and repose. Several of his women could be seen further down the beach – so white it looked like snow – sarongs clinging delightfully to their wet bodies and somehow making them more naked than when wholly unclothed as they sported together in the water, shrieking and giggling as the wavelets buffeted and nuzzled against their tender parts.

It was clear to everyone that they were practising the sweet arts of beguilement on him, stretching their arms up so that the cloth fell away from their breasts, bending and accidentally dropping their sarongs while looking him straight in the eye. How he loved it! Was this not every man's dream and worth all the pain, expense and hostility he had suffered from the jealous and the godly? He must give the girls a few little gifts, show them his favour. Little Rini from Banyuwangi, there, claimed descent from one of the royal houses of Java, a fact that impressed him far less than her sinuous neck and back since he knew the royalty of the Indies to be mostly a bunch of homicidal kleptomaniacs who claimed to redeem themselves only through occasional outbursts of religious lunacy. Delightful. He chuckled and sipped from a bamboo cup of cool coconut water and sniffed the air, washed clean by a thousand miles of clear ocean, then exhaled and relaxed, nodding back into Nature, letting it wash over him, into him, through him. The world was good. Later, he would take a trip across to one of the lesser islands, rowed by his squad of ladies arranged in a nice tableau while thinking of Shakespeare's description of Cleopatra's barge.

And then he opened his eyes and saw a longboat out at sea, pulling in towards them. The world was no longer good. The craft was manned by ragged seamen, dropping their oars and looking at the girls through spyglasses and making rude gestures of invitation and it seemed to him now that those acts of female beguilement he had noticed were directed not at him but at the new arrivals. Some of the girls were responding with waves and giggles and he screamed at them to desist. Didn't they realise they were playing with fire? He was alone and only he could protect them from this floating seascum.

Then he recognised Ross in the bow and watched as he pulled

in and heard him swear at the boatmen, ordering them to stand by their oars or he would flay the backs off them. He and his henchman, Leisk, came striding up the beach, *his* beach, with a clenched, determined look on their faces. Trouble. Vexation. They wore knotted kerchiefs on their heads like silly, comic pirates and stopped a few yards off, looking impertinently at the women, *his* women with blatant lust dancing in their eyes. He had travelled widely in his life but only to seek a place to stop. Now he had found it. This was *his* place and they were defiling it by their mere existence.

Someone had once told him a story about a town where the rich complained that the hungry poor were ruining the taste of their food by sniffing the smell of it outside their big houses. Hare understood that well. The intended moral message, of course, lay in the opposite direction with the endless greed and selfishness of the rich. Asian gods, after all, lived on the smell of food that their worshippers often ate after offering it up to be merely divinely sniffed suggesting that priority was all, that there was plenty for everyone. But eyes and noses were different and he would not allow his girls to be devoured even by the hot eyes of rank flotsam like this. The women would not be bathing here again.

'Good morning, Hare.' No 'Mr' today then and said without deference or a tug of the forelock to one's superior.

Hare nodded, sat back in his chair and closed his eyes again, master of the only piece of furniture and so the world. Whatever was to be said, they were going to have to find the words to say it without his help.

'Have you decided yet how long you will be staying on

Cocos?'

Hare yawned. 'I cannot say. Except that I shall stay on this island of my discovery for as long as it pleases me. Possibly permanently. Possibly not.' He looked up sharply. Ross had positioned himself with the sun behind him so that he could not stare him in the face without being dazzled. 'And when will *you* be moving on with your rag-tag mob?'

Ross ignored that. 'Your people have been coming to my house begging for food. They say the supplies of rice you give them are insufficient. They look half-starved to me. The soil here is too thin to grow crops and no one can survive without supplies shipped in. You've got more people than you can feed. It's got to stop for all our sakes. Overpopulation will kill us all.'

'Half-starved? Damn and blast you, Ross!' He opened his eyes and leaned forward. 'I give them a sufficient allowance. Too many people? Yours will soon outnumber mine and I suggest you ask your mother-in-law about the Lord providing, for you can count on no help from me or my brothers. No doubt she will tell you to trust in Providence whose stark benevolence will, as always, send you famine, plague and war to nicely take care of the excess of mouths among your loved ones. The problem with my own is that they gamble away their ration in cockfighting and *congkak*. Then the winners make the excess into strong drink that leads to further indebtedness and they end up stealing from my stores which makes life precarious for all of us. The only remedy is to cut their allowance to the bone so that they are not tempted to gamble it away, which I have done. But speaking of supplies, I understand from my brothers that you have obtained goods from them on the basis of our being engaged in a joint undertaking of pressing high-grade palm oil. That is both dishonest and illegal. You may expect a letter from my lawyer on the subject. No such agreement exists between us. That is all I have to say on the matter.'

'That was my understanding when last we spoke.' Ross crossed his arms truculently. 'And surely speaking directly is easier than waiting nine months for a lawyer's letter to go each way. It would only be empty bluster anyway, all whereas and wheretofores. Facts is facts and a man's word should be his bond. What's promised can't be unpromised.'

'I spoke only of possibilities at that time. There were conditions and there was no firm engagement on my part. You will be charged for those goods you have rooked my brothers of with accumulating interest.'

Ross put his hands on his hips like an outraged housewife demanding to know where a husband had spent the night. He was a man who had difficulty in keeping his hands out of any conversation, having used them to enforce discipline both on shipboard and on land. Hare had spent the night vigorously with Anna and Maria while Ross would have been with that long streak of misery that was his wife and he smiled at the warm thought, which irritated Ross further.

'Which I refuse to pay as it is the House of Hare as owes *me* money. Know this, then. If it cannot be palm oil, then I have another kind of business in mind – a whaling station. We have a safe harbour, water and wood and boatbuilding skills enough to satisfy the needs of a dozen vessels to come here for supplies, repairs and recreation.'

Hare sat bolt upright, nearly losing his turban and the smile disappeared from his face. A station for refitting and supplying whaling vessels? That would mean attracting hordes of men with sudden money burning a hole in their pockets, men who liked a drink, men who hadn't seen a woman for three years and would soon be off again leaving their consequences behind them – the foulest, rankest gutter slime of the seven seas turned free like uncaged beasts on his own doorstep. Ships were mere nurseries for plague, smallpox, cholera, syphilis. He had a vision of reaching horny hands with dirty nails and leering, scabbed faces set with broken teeth baying for...

'Yes, I thought that would strike home.' Now it was Ross that smiled while Leisk guffawed aloud.

Hare rose to his feet, face suffused with rage. 'This is preposterous. We do not live under any flag but my own so my word is law on this island. As first resident, I totally forbid it. Were you a gentleman, I would challenge you to a duel.'

Ross and Leisk laughed at each other. 'A duel is it? A fancy duel with the overwound son of a clockmaker? And what would be our weapons? Pendulums at dawn? First resident you say? And you forbid it, do you? Then you should get your London lawyer to write a long letter to my London lawyer about it – a very long letter indeed. Hahaha.'

They walked off along the beach, slapping at each other in hilarity, feet sliding in the icing-sugar sand as Ross, in his knotted handkerchief, called over his shoulder, 'By the way, Hare, I love the hat!'

Chapter Five

In Hare's day, Bugis Street would have been a harmless haunt of bloodthirsty, yo-heave-hoing pirates until it was colonised by large numbers of Japanese prostitutes before the First World War. Had they been available, Hare would certainly have wanted one of those for his collection, gift-wrapped in a colourful kimono and mounted on clip-clopping sandals. A major priority of the Japanese occupation had been to ship all these soiled doves back home as injurious to the honour of Japan. Arthur had heard vaguely about the tawdry enticements of the place but never paid much attention to such casual gossip. It was understood that such haunts were intended for the forces – unwashed sailors and rude soldiery, other ranks for the use of – a necessary adjunct to armed conflict like tinned meat and cheap smokes. The Morris was parked with the utmost discretion in a side street. He had already moved it when another car pulled in right in front of him and its driver – a nosy parker – seemed to pay him too much attention. Now he sat in a corner with lowered head though there was surely little danger of any of his acquaintances turning up here to recognise him in the glow of the 10-watt bulbs and he was a silent spectator, cut off the other side of the curtain from where the operatic crowd chorus was performing, made only more lonely by the company of others.

The tight, smoky room was crammed with tars, caps pushed back to tiaras, puffing fag rations, sweating in rude, malodorous health. Come to the East to hide from it here and reduce it to a few crude, physical sensations. Rank others.

The sickly green walls were dotted with curling photos of identical tars, forearms tattooed with anchors and rose-entwined 'Mums', miming ecstatic enjoyment for the camera through glazed eyes. So this was the sleazy underbelly of the beast, the part closest to the bone where life's taste was sweetest. Arthur had sunk so low he was out of his depth. A cockroach scuttled up into a corner by the ceiling and waved its antennae in recognition and confirmation.

They were mostly just boys, pink and unlined, spam made flesh, life having, as yet, not had time to take its hammers and chisels to their optimism. They swore copiously in easy mateship and there was a vigour to their actions that showed an attempt to belie boredom. The tables around which they crowded swarmed with drained Anchor beer bottles, jostling, empty glasses and slops. Their cup ranneth over. Arthur looked into their faces and felt pity at their youth, knowing all the crap they would have to wade through in the course of their lives. At school they had called it dramatic irony.

'May, May! Give us a kiss, luv!'

The proprietress was a muscular Chinese woman piped into a cheongsam that looked under severe risk of splitting like a ripe banana skin who stamped from table to table in time to wailing music from the wireless and energetically urged more beer on them.

'Anchor! Anchor for sailor!'

'Anchors for wankers, luv.' An older sailor mimed a solitary hornpipe eloquently. 'Ay, we've all done it. Stands to treason. Any port in a storm. Especially young Tosh, here.' Tosh, a blond mophead, grinned sheepishly with discoloured teeth and blushed red.

May worked the group, caressed young, beardless chins with comic desire, pinched cheeks, tousled hair, climbed on laps and professionally embarrassed the youngest in front of their roaring mates by gyrating her copious and accomplished backside in their faces till they glowed like embers in the gloom.

'Anchor! Anchor for sailor!' Beckoning more bottles from behind the bar, a rudimentary thing of banged-together bamboo like a cheap stage prop.

Skinny girls drifted in and out and stood around the walls like the bored Nippies in a Lyons Corner House who always yawned and licked their pencils in unwitting eroticism. No licking of pencils here. They were missing a trick.

Someone slid into the chair across from Arthur. She was slight with thick, wavy hair, high cheekbones, pointy chin and almond eyes – very Javanese. She smiled but there was a soft sadness about her young lips and eyelashes that belied the smile and immediately tugged at Arthur's heart. He was astonished at the feeling, a compound of compassion and lust, two elements that the Church had always insisted were immiscible as virtue and vice, giving and taking. He had always assumed that one would banish the other.

He gulped. Was it possible that that was what Eileen had felt for him on those rare occasions towards the end where flesh had met flesh in the grisly rites of marriage? It was certain that pity killed romantic love. But was compassion the same as pity? Didn't the first signify the empathy of equals, the second condescension? He realised he had never thought much about these things. When you were young, love and lust were always within a certain immediate frame and strictly goal directed – scoring, winning, just getting there.

'You buy me a drink?'

Arthur nodded, dazed, called back to concrete things from a world of abstract nouns. Strictly, goal-directed, she waved to May and pointed. Two anchors, not for sailors, appeared with dripping glasses. The girl fastidiously shook drops onto the slurry of beerslops and dust on the floor and poured.

'My name is Salma.' She extended a hand across the table, small but surprisingly strong and hard-boned, in a gesture that seemed oddly formal. Arthur held it and thought of a bird's wing.

'Arthur.' He bit his lip. Too late he realised that perhaps you weren't meant to use your real name in this place of theatre.

'Arfur.' The voice was beguiling, smoky.

He smiled. 'Close enough.' He would spare her the Grimsby business.

'You are not a sailor?'

'Well, I have sailed boats, purely for … No, I'm not a sailor.' They shared a cautious smile, given like a hostage exchange. 'You're from Java?'

'Sort of.'

'So how did you end up in Singapore?'

'So many questions, Arfur. I came to get away, so I could be myself.' She sipped beer and Arthur smiled at her silly foam moustache. She relented. 'Okay. My family wanted to marry me off. I didn't want that so I ran away. Here, it is not so bad. At least I am free. Auntie May looks after us.'

Someone twisted a louder tune out of the knobs on the radio. A popular English love song drooled from the loudspeaker and the sailors began dancing, footslithering over the floorboards to the wireless syrup, some with girls but most cheek-to-cheek with each other in old-fashioned granny-dancing. Tosh seemed to fall asleep on his waltzing mate's shoulder but he sleepdanced on and his face reassumed the glowing innocence of a choirboy. Arthur wondered whether he, himself, would ever feel that free of lingering guilt again, mindlessly content. That must be a happy ship, he thought.

'You are married, I think,' she gestured at his ring. 'But you are not happy.'

'I was married. My wife died.' He was not happy, no.

'Oh. Sorry-lah.'

Tosh's mate had twirled him down tenderly into a chair but was now crouched on both knees and gleefully painting his face with crimson lipstick borrowed from one of the grudging girls – clown's lips, slashed crosses on both cheeks, engorged, throbbing penis on his forehead. Other sailors gathered round, guffawing, loudly offering evil suggestions for further decorative motifs and urging he should be carried to the Taoist tattooist next door, there to be permanently and obscenely inscribed in foreign tongues while still unconscious. What shall we do with the drunken sailor? But, of course, they no longer sang that. Tosh slept trustingly on, dribbling slightly as they ravaged his body with graffiti. Yet his mate's eyes remained soft. The expression of human affection could take so many puzzling and aggressive forms.

'It's very noisy here.' Salma, suddenly decisive, gripped Arthur firmly by the hand. 'Let's go upstairs.' She was wearing some sort of a bracelet that bit into his wrist like handcuffs.

'No. I can't. I'm not sure I …'

She lowered her voice to an urgent whisper. 'If you don't come, May will be angry with me.' She tugged him awkwardly behind her like a lapdog, he half unwilling, half eager on the carpetless stairs. 'Come on! Why else did you come to this place?' She stopped, crestfallen. 'You want someone else, maybe?' Arthur looked at her little, downcast face and compassion surged gallantly again but reigniting another most ungallant desire. Then, unexpected words of wisdom in this thoughtless place. 'You can't just stand around the dancefloor all your life, Arfur. Sooner or later, you've got to start dancing. Is it just me you don't like?'

'No, no, I do like you Salma. It's just …'

It was a nasty, hot, little room, crammed with the detritus of warm-and-serve sexual allure and devoid of all exoticism. Skimpy frocks hung limply on the doors of tired, blue-painted cupboards. Cheap perfumes leaked into each other and fought for breath against the smell of greasy food being cooked in the street outside. Shouts and traffic noise poured in through the open window – Singapore traffic was always a percussion instrument – and somewhere a child screamed as it was slapped with gusto and learned of the unfairness of life. In a corner leant, of all things, a cricket bat covered in unravelling tape, as if discarded by a passing opening batsman but doubtless found useful in cases of self-defence. There was barely room for the bed, a surly iron structure that wheezed like a pthisic poet as Salma sat down on it. No doubt it too had worked hard for a living.

'Come sit.'

Arthur plumped himself down reluctantly on the counterpane and she put her hand on his leg and leant against him. He bumshuffled and looked down.

'Sumba,' he said, surprised.

'What?'

'This cloth we're sitting on. It's a traditional Sumba textile, rather a good one, not a tourist piece!' Arthur's face lit up. He felt a pique of interest revive in him.

'What?'

He was down on his hands and knees, excited, back in familiar territory. 'See. It has some age. It's dyed with traditional indigo and chilli, not modern, chemical dyes, and the thread's hand-spun and the ends – Wow! – finished off with delicate tapestry weave which is really rare nowadays.' He gently smoothed away the impression made by his backside with his hand. 'Oh look, Salma, the lobsters in the pattern are a tribute to the creature's legendary ability to regrow lost limbs and motivate its use in marriage exchanges between groups.' He tugged the other end from under her backside and held it up to the light. 'It really is very finely worked. Ah, and I see that, being natural cotton, it readily absorbs sweat and other bodily fluids and has clearly not faded from excessive washing.'

'What?' Salma laughed and tweaked one edge. 'It's just an old cloth I brought with me from Sabah. I liked the colours. It reminds me of home when I am lonely.

'Sabah? I thought you were Javanese. But I suppose I should have known. You don't speak Javanese English.'

Salma sighed, 'My ancestors came from Java. I was raised in Sabah but my parents are from Cocos. The British shifted us to Sabah when the islands became overpopulated and no one who leaves is ever allowed back by the Ross family who own the place. They say we would cause trouble and bring in new ideas. They don't like new ideas. You will not know about Cocos. Let me explain to you where it is ...'

***

'Can you explain to me, Siti, why nowadays it is always Maria and Anna who come to me at night?' Hare was always at his most irritable in the morning, while sucking his sweet coffee over yellowing teeth, doing the household accounts, seeking accounts of the household. His teeth troubled him nowadays. Sometimes they ached unbearably. He was not looking well. His hair was flyaway with more and more grey among the gold. His eyes were bloodshot. Sometimes he did not change from his night pyjamas into his day pyjamas. What was the point? No unexpected visitor would be dropping by. The morning shave had become something he often neglected, though a man always stood prepared with razor ready – stropped and brush lavishly sudsed – you could not trust one of the women near you with such lethal instruments. And the beard would only grow back. What was the point of fighting that either? On the islands there was no malaria but he seemed permanently tired as if afflicted by it. He looked like a living overdraft.

She lay down the handful of cutlery she was clutching on the linen cloth. 'Mister Alex, it is not of my doing. It is the *congkak*.'

'That damned game again? What has that to do with the company I keep?'

'The African girls are demons of *congkak*. They always beat the other girls and use the debts this causes to have their own way. They rearrange the schedule among themselves. I cannot always be there to stop it. Does it displease you?' She would not mention her own mounting debt to the girls.

'A man does not keep a well-stocked larder in order to eat the same meal every day – even if the dish pleases his palate.' He thought of the sensation of those raised scars against his flesh in the dark, their gangling love lace, a sensuous delight for any blind man. But then there was their continuous and chatting to each other over his body and giggling at jokes from which he was excluded as they worked away at his flesh like a carcase of meat devoid of intelligence. It is distracting and insulting and somehow a violation of the confessional secrecy of the bedchamber, it being part of the gradient of things that they should all know him but only he know them. 'Even my father's London apprentices in clockmaking, a bunch of snotnosed guttersnipes and scabby toerags, had it written into their articles they should not be fed oysters more than three times a week. Even clockmakers dislike excessive regularity.'

Siti smiled with false brightness. 'What if the oysters are freshly cooked and well served and hotly sauced? And does it not mean that the other girls, when they do come, are the more eager to please and more grateful? The game makes their moods more unpredictable. They feel they have won something as opposed to merely doing their duty.' There was pleading in her voice. 'Is that not more exciting for *tuan*?' Siti was clutching at straws and sounded desperate even to herself.

Hare pursed his unshaven lips and mumbled. His mouth was dry. When he woke in the morning it was as if he had crossed the Sahara during the night. There were sticky grains of rice stuck in his beard. 'Well, I grant you there is something to that.' After the recent exactions on his body, he was unsure, for the first time in his life, whether he could cope with a wider assault. The logic of Adam Smith's supply and demand worked its devilish ways not just through his account books but even in sexual matters and, nowadays, he sometimes could not clear his plate let alone lick his platter clean what with this terrible monopoly of the African girls. His dreams were no longer of voluptuous haunches of female flesh but centred mainly on edible meats and his taste for the exotic had fled – solid English delicacies such as steak and kidney pies, plump sausages, great sides of salted ham – while sex seemed less a supreme pleasure than an outrageous tax levied on his flagging manhood. The girls were at him night and day, rolling their eyes and their breasts, touching him as he passed ... His crotch was red and raw. It hurt when he peed. It occurred to him that perhaps they had given him a disease, a dose of Surabaya snakebite or they were slipping something into his food. For God's sake give it a rest. But no, it would not do. He would be master in his own house.

He slammed down his cup on the bamboo table, making it shake. His right hand, he saw, was shaking too and he reached out to steady it with his left. 'Are you all fools? If they constantly win, they must be cheating. Stop the game. Forbid it utterly. No wait, the next time they play, summon me and I will show you all what tricks they are up to and you may take your revenge freely. I have been to some of the best gaming houses in London and Batavia, seen thousands change hands across a green baize cloth on the turn of a single card. I have travelled and seen it all. God knows, I have crapped in a crypt, pissed in a palace and shat in a château in pursuit of experience. A couple of inexperienced bush girls are no match for that.'

Siti looked coy. 'But they use witchcraft, Mister Alex. The other girls say they are witches, creatures of the night. They do not sleep as we do. In the dark they whisper to each other in that language of woodpeckers and their eyes glow like hot coals. Perhaps they are saying spells and attracting demons. We should beat them till they confess. We have had no rain for weeks. It is the African girls' doing. Everyone knows it is so.'

Hare slammed his fist on the table top again, rattling the cutlery in his rage, sending it all flying. 'Damn and blast! A coconut drops on someone's head and it is witchcraft. Or a child falls ill or someone has a bad dream or it rains or it doesn't rain and it is the girls' fault. Blame the tree or the climate or your own almighty god or your own stupidity, not the Africans!' He raised his arms to Heaven. 'Can a man have no peace in his own house even on a desert island?'

Siti crept away, muted and rebuked. But she noticed that all the forks that fell from the table landed with their sharp prongs up. These things did not happen by chance. It must be an omen.

***

They came for him again that night as he knew they would. Hare was plucked from the pit of a troubled sleep by dark and malevolent shapes that he tried in vain to slap away like phantoms of midnight, whining and protesting. The locked door made no difference since they simply broke through the flimsy, woven wall and slid back the bolt and they were already on him with their joint strength, insinuating and clicking like cockroaches, tickling, stroking, licking and frotting, succubus fingers probing his body, before he was fully awake, pulling him down like the sea currents of Christmas Island till his treacherous flesh reacted, only to collapse, like an exhausted racehorse, at the last hurdle, foaming pathetically at mouth not magnificently at groin. Then they melted away laughing contemptuously, leaving him panting, violated and humiliated, ravaged by vampires. Had it been only two of them? In the dark, how could he tell? In the morning it would be just a nightmare. He would tell himself it never happened. But, when he awoke, there was Siti, staring, puzzling at what seemed a giant mouse hole in the wall. The men must not know. Above all, smirking Ross must never find out.

Somewhere, Arthur knew, in Shakespeare or the Bible or the works of Agatha Christie, there was a line about God punishing men by giving them that which they most earnestly desired. The monks that ran his school had used it on him when he was a child and was taking what seemed to his elders an innocent and unchristian pleasure in just being alive. He remembered himself as a happy little schoolboy. When had all that changed?

He had returned from Salma with his virtue unexpectedly intact and having acquired a fine, new cloth for the museum that filled a shocking gap in the textile collection. Salma had been touched to be shown normal kindness and respect and astonished that an old cloth was worth so much money. He had not cheated her but paid a fair price. In theory, it should be regarded as a most satisfactory adventure all round. He had been happy at his find, spread further happiness about him like a radiator dispensing warmth into a cold world ... and yet. He was not fulfilled. Mind and body were at war. He could feel it, a tingling in his very brain. Hare still came like a succubus and stirred his unruly dreams, whispering in his ear of missed opportunities for pleasure, imminent dark events, ticking clocks, the need to seize the day before his mainspring ran down. Sometimes at night, he dreamt of pale and smooth Violet Loo wrestling with dark and wiry Cocos Salma and awoke, bathed in sweat, shamefully tumescent, heart pounding. Was this battle the muted echo of some ancient, racial strife or was it possible they were fighting over him, even if only in their own dreams? He felt torn in impotent loyalty like a mindless football hooligan who fervently supports both teams at a match while both remain quite oblivious to his mere existence. It occurred to him that he was become more a stranger to himself than to Alexander Hare and he was horribly aware that Salma might even draw on the same gene pool as Hare, indeed, given that it was a mere coral rock pool, that seemed almost inevitable. Sleeping with Salma would be supping with the devil, sleeping with Hare himself. How long is a long spoon?

***

At first, a terrible stillness settled over the islands, no breeze, only small, petulant waves that danced on the spot in slick, metallic grey rather than hurling themselves against the coral in blue and white. Then a clotted darkness congealed over the far horizon, the colour of an overripe durian fruit, punctuated by lightning and deafening thunderclaps under an Old Testament sky that sucked up all other light and sound. Mrs. Dymoke fell to her knees and clutched her Bible to her chest like an ailing child, declaring herself a humble sinner who had built on sand but still believed the Lord was a rock.

'He sees our sin. He rides the dark thunderclouds in his infinite justice! Pray for mercy! Pray for salvation!'

Hare's girls were terrified and compulsively recited garbled scraps of the Koran with their cloths pulled over their heads, reminding the deity that they had always been good girls really. There came a sudden blast of sound like a chord delivered on a thunderous cathedral organ with the swell pedal slammed down. The seamen looked out to sea, clutched their mongrel talismans and alone knew what was really coming. If there was a god, whatever his name, then he was a vengeful god and he was heading their way frothing at the mouth with divine wrath.

Hare knew the houses were a deathtrap, built of palmwood and plaited fronds, and too flimsy to protect yet too full of things that would crush and kill. 'Out! Out! Into the trees! There is no shelter or safety here!'

The highest point on the island was only a few feet above the water's edge where they had built for convenience's sake. There was a chance that, if they got to the trees, they could at least find something to hold on to. A terrible wind came roaring in, tearing at the roofs and whirling away barrels and baskets with banshee howls, driving down the flimsy, woven walls and toppling the furniture like ninepins. Hare seized a tangle of ship's ropes and drove his whimpering people out into the teeth and claws of the storm where they lurched over a mix of rough, scrubby grass and bare earth that the Dutch of Batavia would have called a lawn. The slender palms offered no shelter at ground level but there were old, hardwood trees, deep-rooted and solid further in and they struggled through lashing, icy rain towards their open arms, the women screaming and clutching wailing children, the men just as fearful but silently so. Staggering against the gale, stumbling in its pauses, they threaded the ropes into a giant spider's web, round and round between the tree trunks at the centre of the copse, bound the children to their parents with anything they could find, scarves, sarongs, sashes and wedged themselves between the ropes and the hardwoods, crouching away from the storm as the wind tried to rip the breath angrily back from their lungs. Debris of all kinds flew at them as though a giant were clearing house, smashed tables, branches, whole coconut trees crashed against the outside of the little wood. Hare's ironwood throne sailed over their heads and splintered into a dozen pieces. An embroidered sampler, reading 'Home Sweet Home' clouted him maliciously round the ear.

And then the sea came, an implacable wall of water, advancing grimly but with immense power. It swept over the protecting reef and thundered over the beach and surged up to crash down on their heads like an iron bar. Hare found himself back on Christmas Island, choking and spluttering in the hostile surf but the trees stood firm, held him and his people in their embrace, offered the certainty of a continuing solid world at their back as the water drained from his eyes, reclaimed by the eternal sea. Time slowed, stopped dead in the water. It seemed for a moment as if another wave was building in the silent lull and they screamed and braced themselves for the onslaught but it rose only to die abruptly to a mere swirling eddy about their feet. In minutes, the worst was over and time switched back to normal speed. The cold rain was replaced by hot, the temperature of fresh-spilled blood, as the cyclone spat them out and span away and out over the water, indifferent to their fate, feeding and gathering up more strength under its skirts as it raced off across the face of the ocean.

Hare looked around at the shattered world about him – the people shivering and bedraggled, afraid to look up, and unwilling to believe it was past – the vegetation crushed by some divine, great stamping foot. He nodded as if agreeing, at some deep level, the universal ruin. Ogilvie stood there emptily, waiting for him to decide what to make of it all. Ogilvie had been raised as a carpenter with firm but gentle hands and disorder distressed him.

'Luckily only the very edge of the cyclone touched us,' he gasped. 'That could have been very nasty, Ogilvie.' Hare staggered to his feet, clutching at a tree trunk, and laughed as he remembered the words of the Malay sailors on Christmas Island. 'We are lucky the sea was so peaceful today. Sometimes it is rough,' he said. Nobody laughed.

* * *

No wait, that sampler was not from Hare's house. It was from Arthur's own. There it was on the wall over his desk, picked out pedantically in smudged red and green wool by some long-dead, domesticated wifeling. During the war, he had seen too many such slogans, been forced to shout them out himself and was surprised the Japanese officer who had occupied his house had not replaced it with a syrupy view of Mount Fuji. But there it was, another survivor. He and Eileen had bought it in a junk shop in Ely on what passed for a honeymoon. It was supposed to be springtime, the moment when a young man's fancy turns to a fancy young woman, but they spent it in a damp and smoky cottage out in the fens, appropriating for themselves the smug sentimentality of another age. Only later did it take on a slightly bitter and ironic edge as the wolf began to huff and puff and blow their house down.

Singapore was full of people just killing time – conscripts

waiting for the end of their national service, kept wives filling in the dread void before the lunchtime meeting with the girls or the hair appointment, civil servants watching out for the letter finally announcing that long-awaited home posting. In their minds, they lived elsewhere. Time, itself, took on a special glue-like quality. Boredom lay over the expat parts of the city like a smog, so that many enthusiasms were embraced with quiet desperation and drink, sex, shopping, gardening, tennis and swimming were clutched at in the hope of making time loosen and flow.

Worst of all was amateur dramatics. Eileen had early discovered the Gilbert and Sullivan Society. They were typical operetta enthusiasts with cardboard flats and singing to match who got terrible reviews which they blithely ignored and so were never critically endangered. 'HMS Pinafore, just the thing to loosen my apron strings, darling!' Most of the men had been swishily sibilant thespians but with the odd overhandsome stage-strutter, all teeth and codpiece. Not surprisingly, Arthur detested G and S which always went hand in hand with tinkling G and T's. It was the English establishment's smug way of declaring, 'See how cute we are, what sweet and harmless eccentrics. Just look at our famous sense of humour and see how we make fun of ourselves and our most entrenched values – snobbery, nationalism, military violence, elitist art' – as a means of allowing them all to flourish unimpeded. Naturally, only professionals or the wives of officers were allowed to take part in the performance of this story written in celebration of class subversion. The wife of a mere corporal who yearned to be Buttercup was treated like Japanese hogweed and ended up washing costumes. And when he had hesitatingly questioned her about suspected off-stage activities with Dick Deadeye, Eileen had sweetly quoted.

'What, never?

No, never!

What, never?

Well, hardly ever!"

After all, darling, one swallow doesn't make a summer!'

***

'It was the black girls that did it. Witchcraft!'

Sîtî was firm, as the men and girls scoured the lagoon for anything still serviceable. Astonishingly, no one had actually died though many hobbled and limped about what looked like the aftermath of a battle. The lagoon was clogged with palm trunks, ripped up like handfuls of grass. It was fortunate that many of the supplies had been in barrels that were left bobbing in the shallow water intact. Others had ended up nested in the trees like strange fruit. The wells were all swamped with salt water and would have to be laboriously emptied and cleaned.

'They were seen looking out to sea and rattling those antelope horn necklaces they wear, exactly where the storm came from, the day before it all happened. And they do not deny it. When you accuse them, they just smile and look at you with those terrible eyes. They should be driven away to live as lepers with the wild beasts.'

Most of the other girls nodded though the islands boasted neither wild beasts nor lepers – they would make up the minds of the men on the subject later – but not all. Zahara, the sweet-faced, little girl from Pekalongan was equally adamant.

'Not so. This was no human hand. It was Loro Kidul, the goddess of the South Sea, that did it. Even here she can reach us from her shining palace under the water. The sea has no borders, fish are of no nation. Did you not see *Tuan* Hare wearing green clothes on the beach? That is her colour. It is a provocation to her and so she came for him. He has a golden kris that he also wears, taken from the palace in Yogya by the soldiers, that should be returned to her. Did you not see that the great wave sought him out and hit him first? We should take him out to the open sea and offer him up, weigh him down with chains and rocks and throw him over the reef with his kris. It is the only way to save our own lives in this terrible place or she will come again.' Her eyes narrowed. 'But have you noticed? While *we* have lost everything, all our clothes and possessions, this morning those Chinese girls were hobbling around on their pig's trotters, wearing bright new sarongs, were they not? Blood-sucking leeches!'

There would have been *Schadenfreude* elsewhere, of course, the Ross establishment seeing the greater destruction of Hare's household as a mark of their own divine favour, rather as if only having a single leg cut off was to be held a great blessing from on high. It seemed that, for Mrs Dymoke, to be divinely punished was better than to be divinely ignored, yet it was hard for them to feel grateful as she rubbed their status as undoubted sinners in the faces of Ross's people like stinging nettles. For she saw clearly what it all meant. When the big wave hit, she was knocked off her feet and the great, brassbound family Bible she clutched dragged her down like a tombstone. Then, as the water receded, it became an anchor, wedged in the shattered doorframe, preventing her being dragged out to sea. The word of God had been her salvation. The black girls had immediately fled crying to her and stirred up her wrath by revealing how Hare, instead of trying to save them, had cruelly tied them to a tree outside, like sacrificial lambs, to face the full force of the storm with no protection.

'It was only through the great and divine mercy of our Lord God Almighty in his wisdom that any of us sinners were saved from his merited wrath and not cast down into the bottomless pit,' she announced cheerily over the breakfast table as the Ross household wearily spooned in salt-sodden rice. 'And it was surely the power of our prayers that saved Hare and his tribe from total destruction, may they rot in Hell!'

She turned on her son-in-law. 'That Sodom and Gomorrah that is his household cries out to Heaven for righteous punishment and yet we do nothing. We have seen how true is it that our Father maketh his sun to rise on the evil and the good, and sendeth rain on the just and the unjust, as Matthew says in the good book. We must pray, pray, pray. Our own punishment comes from the evil of selling strong drink.'

Ross sighed. He was tired of listening to the old woman wringing out her soul like a dirty mop. 'I've told you before, mother. Rum is part of the sailor's due. If we are to have trade at all, we must sell rum. The Lord changed water into wine in Cana of Galilee and he served it to the apostles in memory of himself. If God wanted us to stop selling rum, he would not have made barrels of it to float.'

'If God had meant us to stay on this god-forsaken island, he would not have sent Hare to plague us.' She looked around nervously at the far horizon. 'Of course, no place is ever really forsaken by God,' she added hastily, 'in his mercy.'

***

Mrs. Barlington-Hughes was a tough, old bird, a culture vulture with a very sharp beak. Widow of a wealthy banker, she sat immovably beady-eyed on the committees of theatres, museums and art galleries, incubating her eggs and viciously protecting her nest from all comers. As head of the G and S players, she saw her primary role as defending Singapore from the works of Wagner, who, as everybody knew, had caused the Second World War. Arthur had ruffled her feathers over funding for the ornithology collection in the past since she regarded pretty Asian birds as merely something God had put in the world to provide adornments for her hats. These afternoon receptions at her rose-clasped mansion in Novena were always the same nightmares of formality and discomfort that were simply about demonstrating how many people her fortune gave her power over. The Geneva Convention meant nothing to her and the proof of her social clout was that so many were obliged to come and be tortured, despite grim foreknowledge, whether they wanted to or not – and most did not.

Outside, the sun blazed on ruthlessly bare lawns that faded away into untamed borders so deep that a whole battalion of unsurrendered Japanese troops might still be lurking in them, waiting to rush out in their boots across the manicured tennis courts that rarely felt even the tender tread of plimsoles. Inside, a minute Chinese pianist in a white dinner jacket and wearing overlarge, implausible dentures tinkled at a piano behind his fixed ceramic rictus and made conversation difficult with crooned Cole Porter showtunes.

'*What is this thing called lerve?*
This funny thing,
Called lerve?'

There were ghastly hors d'oeuvre so small as to be almost homeopathic food – cheese with pineapple, both tinned – boiled eggs on crackers smothered with salad cream, rank fish paste on brittle slivers of toast that cracked in half when you picked them up and tried to put them to your mouth. All over the room, people were cursing and furtively spitting on handkerchiefs and dabbing at fish paste on their clothes and rubbing it into the self-coloured carpet while knocking back the booze – anything to get out of 4/4 time.

Old friends died or went home and you didn't make new ones to replace them and, anyway, at these gatherings there were always more people you wanted to avoid than you wanted to renew acquaintance with. It was certainly pretty much the same, old faces though now with a few more circling Americans, preparing to move in to pick the bones of the dying empire. Behind Arthur, a man proclaimed loudly in a glad-handing Milwaukee accent, 'Johns, toilets, that's the future for Asia. Yes, sir! A hundred million brown and yellow aaaases out there crying out for ceramic bathroom fittings and not those two-skidpads-and-a-hole gizmos. Asians don't know squat about toilets. Har, har, har!'

Arthur turned his back, feeling a rare twinge of outraged patriotism. It was a small but welcome justification of the British presence to make one's way to some remote hill station and there find a Victorian sanitary apparatus still doggedly flushing after nearly a hundred years' faithful service to Queen and Country – indeed in blissful indifference to the sex, race or religion of either the monarch or its humbler patrons like British justice itself. The Roman Empire had left the pomp and thunderous magnificence of the Roman Catholic Church as its monument. With the British Empire, it would be travelling companies performing Shakespeare in Tamil for the British Council and the more parochial but friendly hiss of Twyford Adamant cisterns. Independence would be less a watershed than the continuity of a water closet.

He went and stood, isolated in a bay window, already on his third G and T, the bitter tonic water matching his mood, repelling boarders with baleful glares.

> '*I was a humdrum person,*
> *Leading a life apart,*
> *When love flew in my window wide,*
> *And quickened my humdrum heart.*'

'Hello, Arthur.' Macclehose, beer gripped in manly fashion, showing bleached, non-ceramic teeth. The very last person he wanted to be trapped into conversation with, the bastard standing there in shorts, firm-thighed, trying to show cool sophistication like co-respondents in some Noel Coward play. What was his first name? Norman. Were they even on first name terms? How could anyone have a lover called Norm? Arthur, wielder of a mighty sword, valiant warrior for people and faith? Yes. But Norman? No. Didn't Arthur fight Normans? No that was Anglo-Saxons. Arthur downed his gin and tonic, reached for another from a passing tray.

'Sorry to hear about Eileen by the way. I don't think I actually ever said it.'

A gear engaged and crashed in Arthur's brain. 'Hear?' He clenched and swallowed. 'What *I* hear is that you just happened to be there, in the Genteng Highlands at the time, that you *saw*. You were a witness.' He tried to put a note of steel in his voice and make it sound judicial but it came out weirdly ecclesiastical.

*'But after love had stayed a little while
Love flew out again.'*

'Me? Sorry, old man, you're on the wrong track there. I was in KL, regional conference on delivery of rural health care. Evaluation of services provision. Ask anyone.' He nodded at the glass and sneered, secure in his alibi. It was obvious to Arthur that the two of them had arranged a rendezvous somewhere up in the hills. 'Maybe it's on the grapevine that you're hearing things these days, Arthur. Hitting the bottle a bit too much? Natural enough given the circumstances but I'd slow down a bit if I were you. If I'd been a witness, I'd be dead too, wouldn't I? Stands to reason.'

Wouldn't that be a shame? Arthur swigged like a Viking draining an alehorn, thrust out his jaw in defiance, crushed lemon pips fearlessly between his teeth. Macclehose's own wife had been a pathetic little mouse creature and fled home a couple of years back, sucked dry by the heat, dreaming of chill rain. Now she would probably be sitting in Dorking prattling about missing the wonderful climate out here.

'Is that what you call it these days, services provision?' Arthur snorted. 'Did you think I didn't know about you and Eileen? Everybody knew.' He reached for another passing gin and tonic.

'Keep your voice down, you damned fool. Don't make more of a spectacle of yourself than you already have.'

'And just what do you mean by that?' Arthur checked himself. Tears started to his eyes. A spectacle? He and Eileen had been a pair of spectacles.

> *'Just who can solve its mystery*
> *Why should it make*
> *A fool of meee?'*

A superior expression settled on Macclehose's broad, already-smug features. 'Eileen told me all about you and what you get up to. She told me how you neglected her and spent all your time with your fancy women. Your collection of fancy birds, she called it. She said you had a whole harem of fine-feathered friends at the museum. She always laughed about it. She was such a plucky little thing.'

> *'You took my heart*
> *And threw it away.'*

'But that was just a joke, our own little joke,' he gasped. There was a terrible betrayal in her sharing it with this clown ... but perhaps she was just laughing at his stupidity and it was still a bond between them that he didn't understand it. 'Just a silly ... Oh, this is too idiotic ...' Why was he even defending himself to this buffoon when he was the wronged husband who should be doing the shouting and ranting and throwing down challenges? He felt a wave of anger bearing him up that he seized and rode like a Californian surfer.

'You weren't the only one, you know. There were others,' he crowed. 'Plenty of others. And she always came home to *me*.' Somewhere, he had seen a film where someone clicked his fingers contemptuously in a rival's face so he did that and threw in an ironic bark of laughter for good measure. Gin slopped down his trousers.

> *'... That's why I ask the Lord in heaven above*
> *What is this thing, this funny, funny thing*
> *What is this thing called lerve?'*

The pianist ended with a great high hand flurry, stood and bowed to non-existent applause, before scurrying off to the kitchen for refreshment.

Macclehose leaned in, holding his mouth too close so that Arthur felt his spit dampen his forehead. 'Laugh if you like, you swine,' he hissed like a film villain. 'I've a mind to knock you through that bloody wall. You didn't appreciate Eileen. She was wasted on you. Pearls before swine.'

'Tears before bedtime.' Why had he said that? But it did the trick. Macclehose inflated slowly like a puffer fish and Arthur drew back his fist to strike. He had led a life where passion was always subjugated to intelligence. There had been the war, of course, but that had been a licensed mayhem where he had been swiftly reduced to passive suffering on the sidelines, the quietest of heroism, and he had easily reverted to peacetime ways at its end. He had not hit anyone since he was twelve years old when his ownership of an adored Dinky Toy sand truck was contested by a bigger boy at school. That had ended in bloody noses all round and a good caning thrown in to show that others possessed exclusive rights over his violence. Perhaps this was the time to take them back as a true grown-up. What would Hare have done? Shot him with a blunderbuss probably. He had no blunderbuss. The technicalities of fisticuffs momentarily escaped him. Should he put down the glass first? No. Macclehose held a glass too and 'glassing' he believed to be a recognised move in the repertoire of contemporary street fighting. But did the thumb go inside the knuckles or outside, the fist vertical or horizontal? He vaguely remembered being told to twist as he thrust, putting his weight on the front foot and prepared the confusing sequenced manoeuvre in his head as he had once learned to bayonet sandbags in the militia. Unfortunately, Singapore had not been invaded by sandbags.

'Now, now. What are you two boys arguing about? You're behaving like an old married couple, haha.' A booming voice and calming, meaty hands laid on their office-thin arms, unknotting the unconvinced muscles. Mrs. Barlington-Hughes was there, wearing an example of the vast surplice-type garment that missionaries once promoted as indispensable for the prevention of lust – just the sort of thing Hare's African girls would have worn – in her case an unnecessary ingenuity. 'Politics, I'll be bound.' She waved a wearily remonstrative finger, clanking the heavy jewellery round her neck – the sort of jewellery you would put on a horse. Her hair sported a helmet of cast-iron waves by Richard Hudnut. 'All this independence nonsense, is it? Everywhere it's the same. People are getting so upset. I expect it'll all blow over. The locals will never get on without us. They'll be at each others' throats inside a year and begging us to come back and take over to sort it all out again. You'll see.' She laughed and dropped her voice to breathe a great secret in a prophetic voice that echoed around the room. 'Do you know, there was even a suggestion that all us members of the Farquhar Museum board should be swept away and replaced completely by new, local appointees. Just imagine! What nonsense!' She clutched the diamonds at her own throat and rolled her eyes. 'I soon put a stop to *that*. They'll be wanting to get rid of the Queen next.'

'No chance of that.' Oleaginous Battersby was there spreading oil on troubled waters through smirking beaver teeth. 'I think everyone appreciates the benefit of maintaining a link.' He nodded slowly and heavy-headed like a man who had acquired sad wisdom unwillingly but inevitably, the way a boat accumulates barnacles. 'You'll find the hotheads soon calm down when they get a little experience of real power and the problems it brings. A vision is easy to sustain only when it's embattled. They don't seem to appreciate the sheer amount of work we have to do.'

He turned to Arthur. 'By the way, the repatriation johnnies say you haven't been in touch yet, Grimsby. Learn from Christmas, old man. Don't leave it too late and get caught up in the rush to get your tree up. There's always more to sort out than you think and we don't want any last-minute fuss and mess. Got to keep things nice and tidy, haven't we? And there's always your chap – what's his name? – Bok Ong to consider. I hope you've made proper provision. A bit cruel of you to make him keep on working at his time of life, if you don't mind my saying so.'

Arthur was genuinely stunned. 'What's this? He won't stop. I've tried. But Bok? *My* Bok? How on earth do you know about him?'

Battersby waved airily. 'Oh, don't ever forget the little people and don't underestimate what we know. The Special Branch are no fools and I keep my finger firmly on the pulse. I was looking through some old security files the other day, sorting out what to leave and what to burn. You wouldn't believe some of the things ... Well, anyway, lots to do, you see. Never ends. When you toddled off to sit out the war in Changi, he stayed on with that Jap who took over your place and kept his eyes and ears open and sent a steady stream of gen off to our chaps in the jungle at great personal risk. Nearly got a gong for it except the Hon. Gov. thought we were dishing out too many in one go and that might devalue the currency. After that, it all sort of got lost in the works somewhere. I thought you knew.'

The pianist returned, blotting his lips with a hankie, and

bowed deeper to presumably even louder non-existent applause, then struck up again with pace.

> 'When your instinct tells you that disaster
> Is approaching you faster and faster
> Then be like the bluebird and sing
> Tweet, tweet. Tralalalalala ...'

***

Zahara sat alone at the wooden frame and drew a long, curling line across the stretched, white cloth. From the blank void, she coaxed out tendrils and flowers, swirling leaves and cascading petals as in a primal act of creation worthy of Brahma and Shiva, outlining them in molten brown wax from the *canting* cup she held lightly in one hand. The speed of movement was crucial, too fast and the solid line would become mere dots, too slow and blobs would form. She had learned to measure smooth, slow time like this, with her hands, since the age of six, sitting on her mother's lap, snug and secure in her village, drawing the world in negative, since dye would not stick to the waxed areas. Then had come the failed harvests, the call from the big house that her parents could not refuse, the ejection after the death of her master.

In Java, flowers sprang from the volcanic soil like weeds, forcing their way through the rioting greenery. Here, on this blank island, there were none to be seen until she made them, for flowers were a luxury the thin, grudging soil could not afford. As they emerged from the tight weave, it was as if they brought their sudden fragrance with them to throb in the air around her and she breathed it in gratefully, her eyes moist with the memory of loss. Now a bird hovered over a trembling frangipani on fluttering wings. A butterfly rested, weightless, on a stem, its wings to be slashed later with bars of red and yellow as she dipped the cloth into the dyes in the slow, laborious process of colouring in, scraping, rewaxing, redipping until the cloth blazed with all the shades of the rainbow. The *naga* sea monster's tail began in the top left corner, snaking sinuously through the foliage, gripping and tearing with its dragon's claws towards the bottom right. She patiently etched in the overlapping scales like armour, one by one, and her deft fingers picked out the razor-sharp teeth in the gaping mouth, supporting the hot, wet, lolling tongue that steamed in her mind. The Chinese merchants said the *naga* controlled rain and floods and storms and some were reluctant to buy dragon cloths at home, or even claimed that they were reserved for rulers and emperors so not for common men but here there was no such impediment to her art. She paused, looking at the empty face, then began on the reptilian, hooded eyes with their coldly sliding membranes, inking around the pupils, the act that brought the beast to consciousness and life. Her hand shook a little. The wax had cooled and needed reheating over the fire and seemed to be resisting her designs. The creature stared stolidly back at her, then suddenly stirred, flexed and rippled its powerful spine, spread its jaws and winked. It was done.

Chapter Six

Alexander Hare waded out into the moonlit lagoon and took simple delight in the golden iridescence thrown up by his feet. Crushed coral always formed a sort of lacework between the high and low tidemarks but now the sea was steadily throwing back half-digested debris from the cyclone. Just a few feet out, it was still soft, caressing sand underfoot, gentle and unblemished and he pushed out further and released his body into the water, the sea taking him in a wash of wellbeing and buoying him up in a weightless cradle. The slow, rhythmic immensity of the ocean absorbed his fluttering concerns.

It was good to be alone, away from the women with their jealousies and constant importunities. 'Give me a new sarong!' 'Give me a new sash!' 'Why did you give Jasmin a pin for her hair and me nothing?' 'Why do you never send for me anymore?' 'Why do you drive us out in the sun to press oil so we become dark and ugly like the black girls?' 'Why don't the Chinese girls work outside like we do? If their feet are bound so they cannot walk on sand, that is not our fault.' Sometimes he felt he was a lizard trapped in a storm gutter and being eaten alive by swarming ants.

He sighed and ducked his head under the cool water, washing

away his cares and responsibilities, feeling the delightful tickle of the water around his naked genitals. His body was becoming flabby and pear-shaped. He was turning into his father. The girls were chubbing up too and becoming lazy. Perhaps there should be compulsory morning naval drill on the beach. There was trouble back in London and Calcutta with trading houses falling like dominoes, a cyclone of unpaid debt engulfing them and dragging them down. His brothers had lost money in a bank collapse. Trade was bad, insurance was up, cash money was in short supply and paper too dominant with all the world's silver ending up in China where they sold much and bought little. The House of Hare was suddenly wobbly and money was short. His brothers insisted he must spend less and earn more from the oil business. He had never learned to fear God but now he suddenly feared everything else.

He groaned and turned on his back, soothing the tight muscles of his neck and shoulders and looked up at the peachy-hued moon that the Muslim girls claimed as their own. It seemed bigger here as if it had expanded to allow for the bigger sky. The Chinese had something or other about the dark patches up there being hares. It etched the palm trees along the shoreline in sallow light but indistinctly, so that his mind filled in the blanks from memory and turned them into English oaks lining an English village. He had just made matters worse by playing *congkak* with the black girls. They had humiliated him, cleaned him out, twinkled every coin out of his breeches and that had made them arrogant and the other girls jealous. But where would they spend their money? They were the fools. He turned his neck and let out a scream of bubbled frustration into the water.

Suddenly, there was something new going on. He was aware not just of the swirling, indifferent flow of water and weed. He had learned to swim unhandily, one summer, in one of the Hampstead ponds with his brothers and was used to kicking against underwater plants. Once, he had become entangled and barely escaped drowning, coming up for the third time, to see them pointing and laughing, taking it all for a joke as he fought to live and there had been other times since, on board ship and on Christmas Island, that, he feared, foretold the manner of his dying. But this was different. Here was something exploring him tentatively, something horribly purposeful and *alive*. It brushed his flailing legs, returned to appraise his back, then grabbed determinedly at a foot, then a shoulder, yanking him down.

His first thought was a shark and terror flared through him. But here were no ripping teeth, no silent bombburst of blood up through the water. It felt like hands! He yelled and kicked out, connected to something hard, struck out for the shore, felt himself pulled back, inhaled water and choked. He lashed out with arms and legs blindly into the dark water, broke free, made for the beach, realised too late that he was heading the wrong way and out towards the steady roar of the surf. Never mind, there was a rock there, uncovered at low tide and he hauled himself aboard it shaking and sliding, cutting his hands and legs on barnacles, not caring, anything to be free of the water and whatever was down there. He lay panting, hugging the comforting solidity of the rock, his mind running wildly, speculating what might be lurking in the iron-black water. Could it be a giant octopus? Surely that would leave marks from its suckers on his arms and legs. Anyway, they were deep water creatures. It *felt* so human. Could it be? His eyes ran along the blur of the shoreline. Did he see movement there at the foot of the trees or was it just a trick of the light?

After a few minutes he began to feel chill. He knew he had to return to the sea. There was no alternative if he wanted to get back to home and safety and already the level of the water was creeping up the sides of his refuge as the tide came in. Heart pounding, he slid his body back into the sea, the salt water burning at his cuts and swam with silent, tremulous strokes, body electrically alive and holding his torso as far out of the water as possible, knowing relief only when his feet grounded and he staggered ashore. Palm fronds whispered in the velvet night and a screech of female laughter came from the house. He stamped grimly up the beach and burst through the door.

Siti screamed. Like Mary Shelley's Prometheus tearing knowledge from a hostile universe, he raged into the light of the smoking lamp that hung from the rafters, wild-haired, wild-eyed, streaked with blood and stark naked. The other girls shrank back in shame and terror and gathered their sarongs about their bodies and hid their eyes. Hare grasped his own knuckles and gibbered – a madman-drool trickling down his chin.

'Which one of you was just outside? Who was it?'

The girls looked at each other in puzzlement. Conversation buzzed in various tongues. Finally, Siti spoke up. 'No one, *tuan*.' She spoke quietly, denying his own passion, as if to a desolated child. 'We have all been here together. All evening.'

He looked around, counted. They were all present. They were

lying, of course. It was a conspiracy. Hair! Whoever it was that had tried to drown him would still have wet hair. He seized the lamp angrily from its hook and shone it in their lying faces, hands shaking, circled and studied them all. Shadows danced around the walls. They all had wet hair.

'How? Why?'

Anna smiled up at him with sweet innocence as she patted dry the long, straight tresses of the youngest Chinese girl. 'What is the matter? What has happened? We have all been here together. We have been washing each other's hair. You look as if you have been washing your hair too but you should rinse it now in fresh water or it will dry stiff with salt. It feels so good, doesn't it?' She waggled her shoulders beguilingly and grinned at Maria. Her companion reached forward and flicked the end of Hare's penis to screams of girlish laughter, like a chorus of cats.

He slammed down the lamp and stamped out into the night. It's hard to look anything but silly when you are a naked male. It's something to do with the way men's genitals wobble when they walk.

***

Arthur was horribly aware of his own body, feeling as exposed as a mouse on a town square. It was a private thing, not for public exhibition and he had come ill-prepared. He had got as far as taking his shirt off and suddenly noticed how unattractive his torso was – pink, mottled, flabby. Now he was turning, not into his father but his grandfather and he felt the full absurdity of sensuality in one not young and where it was unredeemed by beauty. But this was a commercial arrangement, not an affair. What was it someone had said at the club? 'You're never too old and too fat, just too poor.' So looking terrible was no impediment. Still ... a spare tyre hung over the waistband of his Y-fronts like the tongue of a lapping dog making him think of floppy spam fritters hissing in a pan at a NAAFI canteen. His toenails he knew to be a disgrace. He had not plucked his nostrils. Fortunately, the shutters were clapped up against the harsh noontime heat, slicing the world into blades of light so that full forensic disclosure of his awfulness was prevented. On the other hand, Salma was extended on the bed beside him, skirt riding up over slim, languorous legs that he yearned to see more clearly – golden, firm-muscled, as smooth as waxed paper. He shuffled off trousers and slid beneath the concealing sheet, drawing it up hastily over his breasts in a way that reminded him of how the Chinese assistants treated the public viewing of a body at the morgue with the theatrically insincere performance of respect required by family onlookers.

'I don't expect you to come back, Arfur. Quiet ones never do, you see. They think too much and don't listen to their bodies talking. May was surprised, too. And she is never wrong.'

'Perhaps I wondered if you had any more Sumba cloths to sell.' He had pondered the ins and outs – unfortunate phrase – of returning for days – and nights – pictured it in his head, pumped out desire and retreated into shame only to have desire return strengthened and refreshed.

'Where is Auntie May?'

'It is Sunday. She goes to the temple for her blessings and the church for her sins.'

Salma stood and slipped out of her dress in one smooth movement like an eel shedding its skin and wriggled sinuously renewed under the sheet so that her young warmth flowed into him like healing balm. He had forgotten what a beautiful, young, human body looked like and was intrigued by the reptilian knobbles of her curved spine. She pulled a pin from her topknot to release a torrent of scented hair. Cloves, jasmine. Arthur hesitated then slipped his arm around her, worried to be tumbling so quickly from animal lust to human affection. He realised that what he had missed from Eileen was not sex but warm physical touch and that, all his life, he had had sex with people for the greater pleasure of going to bed with them – something not permitted under the strictures of Moses but common enough in the East.

Salma didn't have much in the way of breasts, certainly, but he had always regarded an obsession with breasts as grossly infantile, being more of an engine-room kind of man himself. With Eileen, there had been a recognised series of steps up the sexual ladder, a standardised back and forth, that led to a satisfactory and familiar conclusion, all rounded off with a cup of tea, served by him, with two sugars. Here, he was an actor lost without a script. Salma's youthful shoulders were irresistible, slim but angular as pelican wings, sweet, toffee-coloured, lightly dewed with sweat like fruit fresh-picked in the cool of morning. He licked and tasted delicious salted caramel on his tongue. That was not in the Eileen G and S script but a whole different production. Salma's mouth was wide and generous beneath his own so tight and pinched, the lips plumped velvet against his own of thin bacon rind. Bacon. What was it Francis Bacon had said? 'There is no excellent beauty that hath not some strangeness in the proportion.' For God's sake Arthur, stop thinking, just feel!

She giggled as if at his thought. That was not in the script either. He was agreeably surprised how personal, how *kind*, such a humiliating encounter as this could be. His imagination had got it all wrong. For, what should be a mutually demeaning act of colonial exploitation, seemed to offer the opportunity of real human contact. Tears started to his eyes. Why should the perception of beauty make you cry? He was aware that, for the first time in years, he had an unscripted erection hard enough to knock nails in with and, emboldened, reached lower and froze. There was another one down there.

'What the ...?'

He pulled back, aghast, as from contact with an electric eel. He had not touched another man's cock since school – that same bigger boy he had ended up punching. Now, how had all that come about? His mind tried to slither off down that distracting snake. But that was not the most pressing issue at the moment.

'You have a ...' he groped desperately for the Malay slang, 'bird.'

Salma, now firmly revealed as Salman, sat up brightly, pushing back the sheet. 'Yes, a bird and two eggs.' Said proudly, self-exhibiting. 'Did you not know? It is the speciality of Bugis Street. Many charge extra but I do not. So, it is what you call an unexpected bonus for you.'

Salman reached out and tweaked playfully, clearly intending to resume operations but Arthur's own bird had gone into a tailspin and only his worst fears were now aroused. He backed away, nearly falling out of bed.

Salman frowned, puzzled. 'What is wrong, Arfur?' He looked down. 'Mine is a very good one I think.'

It was true. Had it been some ancient Hindu artefact, carved in basalt, Arthur would have enthused over its aesthetic virtues as a work of high museum quality, the perfect, smooth symmetry of the shaft, the delicate *Art Nouveau* curves and curlicues of the bare head and the fineness of moulding of the testes. It would have been an object of veneration not a weapon of offence and he would have enjoyed crafting a label and designing an artful mount. The circumcision had been expertly executed with no cutting of corners and he would have had to run appreciative fingers over it and hold it up to the light to celebrate the way the artist had sculpted the soft sheen of the surface and the calculated fall of shadowing. It would have led him to muse – Hare-like – on the Australian habit of subincision, causing the erect penis to open like a flower, or the Bornean insertion of a piercing crossbar or the Thai practice of setting small metal bearings under the skin of the rod. Perhaps he would have remarked on the fine patina of use. All proof that sex didn't just happen between the sheets. It happened inside your head.

'I'm sure it's received the highest praise – deserves a standing ovation ...' He backed out of the bed, grabbing at clothes, stubbed his toe painfully on the cricket bat – a timely reminder of the manly virtues of school – and hopped leg before wicket into his trousers. 'An excellent piece, yes, in itself. I can see that. But you see, it's just not what I had in mind. It's a little unexpected – being there where it is. I'm sorry, Salma. I just don't think I can make the necessary adjustment.'

***

'Do you know what it is like to play with a man who is young and beautiful, someone you are perhaps in love with? Do you know it is possible to love a man's ears and fingers? His touch would fill you with fire.' Maria had formed a sort of lecture group, the girls clustered around her feet like chicks around a hen. 'I have known it once, when I ran away and lived in the mountains in Africa, before they caught me and dragged me back. There was such a man.'

Translation was a laborious process that diluted the force of her words – English to Javanese and Malay and Chinese like a snake wriggling its way through a maze. She waited and resumed only when the Bengkulu girl fell silent. But despite the delay, their faces were still eager and wild-eyed and she knew she held them in the palm of her hand.

'It is unbelievably sweet. Sweeter than honey.' Perhaps they would not know want honey was. 'Sweeter than palm sugar. You lie awake at night with the blood pounding in your ears. You think of no one else. Was there not someone in your past like that? It does not have to be someone you lived with. Perhaps you never even spoke to them, only saw them from afar, a boy in the street, a man at the mosque, glimpsed just for a moment and then swallowed up. But somehow you never forgot them.'

A dreamy expression had come over their faces. Some of them let their mouths hang open. One began to sob. She struck home.

'There is a ship in the harbour. Today, there are other men on the island who are not Alexander Hare, kinder men, younger men, stronger men – handsome men of every race and colour. You should meet them. Perhaps the man you try to think of when Hare touches you is among them.'

The women turned to each other.

'Men only want one thing …'

'But it's even worse when they don't.'

'It is true that *Tuan* Hare neglects us. When we go to him at night now, he just lies there and snores.'

'Look at this rag I am wearing! When I ask for new clothes, he just looks the other way and pretends not to understand.'

'White men are all tight-fisted. The Dutch are so mean they do not even throw their own snot away but store it in cloths in their pockets till they are stiff enough to make soup.'

'He says we must go out to the other islands and live there like wild pigs to collect more coconuts to make oil like the others.'

'He is always angry and asking questions. Now, he carries a knife ever with him and keeps it under his pillow at night. I lie awake in the dark and listen for his breathing and shake and shake if I cannot hear it, for what could happen if he has a nightmare and I cannot quickly calm him?'

'He makes me taste the food I bring him before he will eat it. It is not proper for a wife to eat before her master. And always he guzzles salt pork. What is a good Muslim girl to do? I tell him so and he shouts at me.'

'Here is so boring! We are not allowed to go to the other settlement. We have no family. In Java it was lively.'

They turned to Maria. 'How may we meet these people? Is it safe? How may we do it without *Tuan* Hare knowing? If we made him angry would he not punish us?'

Maria exchanged a knowing smile with Anna. How stupid these girls were that they would hold onto these small resentments and cower before these silly fears and simply not see the overwhelming outrage of being *enslaved* to this man who owned them like dogs. They accepted it, tried to create normal lives out of the fragments of pain.

'I have a plan. I will show you the way.'

***

Arthur was shaken by the Bugis Street experience. It was all a bad joke, a silly lark, by God or perhaps the ghost of Hare that he did not find at all funny. It was ultimately all Hare's fault, of course, driving him out of his own skin, making him do things he had never done before just *because* he had never done them before. Salma/Salman had been a step too far, several steps too far. Carrying on like this was not the mark of a mature adult who knew himself and his place in the world, he had reverted back to being some maudlin teenager who found every prefigured slot irksome and questioned the quiet, received orthodoxies that ruled the world. And the world seemed to find it not so much refreshing as irritating. Yet this was no time to change course. He knew he was running wild and oddly proud of it.

Violet Loo walked through the door of his office like a gliding Edwardian belle in a finishing school exercise, cup in extended hand instead of book balanced on head, careful of slopping the contents into the saucer.

He looked up. 'Coffee, Miss Loo. You know, I rather think I'd like to have coffee, not tea, from now on. Just for a change.'

'You wha'?' She stopped suddenly. The tea, uninformed, kept going and slopped, a storm in a teacup.

'I said I think I'd rather have coffee than tea in future if that can be arranged.'

She gaped, glared. 'I just buy tea. Kennot-lah. Also is rich *tea* biscuit. Say so on packet.' She extended the saucer to show two biscuits dissolving richly in slopped tea. 'See?'

'I can eat a rich tea biscuit with coffee, can't I? Or would the biscuit police come and take me away?' He smiled boyishly.

Violet did not appreciate this unusual waggishness. She sighed, exasperated, slapped the tea down on his desk and walked off throwing her hands up in the air. 'Aaagh! Siao!' Finger twirling at her temple to signify craziness. 'See how. Maybe can buy rich *coffee* biscuit but don' promise. Wah lau eh!'

***

'St. Andrew's day. The day of your local god, isn't it, Mr. Leisk?' Maria had formed a syncretic and pragmatic view of Christianity through encountering it in many of its divine forms.

Leisk laughed. 'You'd best not let Mrs. Dymoke hear you say that, lassie. But there's some truth in it. We'll be celebrating tonight with Scottish country dancing – "The Bees of Maggieknockater" and "The Duke of Atholl's Reel".' He jogged from foot to foot in demonstration, shaking each as if it had bells.

A ramshackle ship was moored a little way out from the beach, rigging rotting, sails torn and unhandily stitched, stinking to high heaven of putrid fish – a typical whaler. Its loathsome, sweet stench of decay washed over the whole settlement, worse even than that of a slave vessel and a pool of rancid oil had settled around its keel. Men were rolling barrels of water down the beach back to dinghies while others further out were hauling them aboard, all engaging in an appropriately ragged shanty. They were mostly young, of an age, she thought, where men have more blood than sense in them. In confirmation, they stopped, gawped at Maria despite the lust-smothering shroud she was wearing, then the sudden silence was filled with shouted blatant invitations as they roared with laughter and stale appetite. One did a very naughty, unnautical jig on the foredeck involving pelvic thrusting and fist-pumping to the delight of his companions.

They would do nicely. 'Is that Scottish country dancing, Mr. Leisk? Then I think the girls should like to come to your feast. Perhaps you would like to buy some rum to make everyone happy. I have money.' She held out a fistful of coins.

Leisk rubbed his chin, looked at the money, looked at Maria. His mouth was dry. He was suspicious. Things like this just did not happen in the world as he knew it. But then, every sailor had heard about the free love of Tahiti and they had the same palm trees here too. There wasn't a vessel where it wasn't talked about.

'And Mr. Hare. What does he say to that?'

'I think you have a saying, "What he doesn't know can't hurt him." He is away on another island in charge of the men working there, harvesting nuts. He will not return for a week with his nuts. Mr. Ogilvie is in his place but he spends his time with his wife at the other end of the island and she has something that will make him sleep.'

Leisk shook his head. He mumbled, half to himself. 'Mr. Ross would not like it. Mrs Dymoke would rage like a wildcat.' He was sweating, panting a little. She was a bold little missie right enough. He looked around nervously.

'They don't have to know, either. You must decide are you a cock or a hen, Mr. Leisk? But think of all the Scottish dancing you can have.'

The men had gone resentfully back to work under the lashing tongue of an officer, just letting out the odd muffled catcall and whistle in their direction behind his back, making a game of hide and seek out of it.

Leisk rubbed his jaw. His voice was hoarse. 'It cannot be here.'

'I shall bring the women to the southern beach where it is quiet. No one will know. At low tide, tonight.'

He furtively looked around and grabbed the money, an aroused Judas, stuffing it into his shrinking pocket. Ross's women must not know or they would come at them, Bible-bashing. Perhaps the cock would have time to crow twice before the denials of dawn.

***

Solomon Da Cunha sat at Arthur's desk where once a Japanese officer had sat and drummed his fingers on the scarred worktop.

The essential difference was that the Japanese was going, Da Cunha had just arrived and he was 'getting the feel' of the place. There had been much pushing and shoving over the racial allocation of different jobs, the need for balance and harmony. A Malay, as a son of the soil, would have been the best choice to officially reign over Nature and History, though there were many more Chinese that could wave paper qualifications at you. But a Eurasian was felt to be the most suitable cultural bridge in a period of transition, embodying both faces of the coin. It had been tossed, caught and come down firmly and predictably Da Cunha.

Arthur, displaced, sat across on the same hard chair he had sat on to discuss Kafka and the contemporary sense of alienation with the Japanese so many years before. History was just musical chairs.

'So where's the best place for Portuguese grilled fish round here?' Da Cunha, like most of Portuguese heritage, was basically Indian but crammed into a horribly hot Western suit of skimpy cut. He drawled his vowels as if reluctant to let them go, something he must have learned up at the Raffles Institution.

Arthur had long formed the opinion that Eurasian food was exactly the same as that eaten by everyone else except for the word 'Portuguese' in front of every dish.

'Oh, I expect you'll find it in the hawker centre down the road. They do all the usual. I generally make do with a sandwich in the office. It saves time and bother.'

Da Cunha sniffed.

'Would you like to go through the morning mail with me and get the hang of how we do things?'

Da Cunha looked down wearily at the great pile of correspondence stacked by his elbow. 'Oh no need for that. I'm sure I'm quite capable of answering a letter without help and I'm happy for you to carry on until the transfer of power is complete. After all, there can't be much to do around a museum apart from giving it a good dusting every few years but I will need a bigger desk. In fact, I will need a much bigger office. I was thinking we might get rid of some of those boring, old, stuffed birds once you're gone and free up some room. Our foremost goal must be the education of the popular mind out of its colonial set and it is important that they see their new leaders installed in an appropriate style. We shall have to change the name of this place of course. Farquhar allowed slavery and drug-dealing in Singapore. He kept concubines. No wonder they called him the *Rajah* of Malacca. Most unsuitable. He will have to go. That Company coat of arms in the historical section will have to go too. History must be kept up to date.'

No more *Auspicio regis et senatus Angliae*. No more 'by the authority of the English King and Parliament'. Arthur had little Latin, just enough to ensure medical unintelligibility before the layman, and now, it seemed, the datives were restless tonight. What if they had named the museum after Alexander Hare, the Sultan of Mokolo? Arthur opened his mouth to protest. After all, Da Cunha himself was a monument to historical miscegenation with one of those noses that only ancient Greek statues have – set up high between the eyebrows and coming straight down like a blade, as if trying to keep the eyes from seeing each other. Hare would have wanted one of those for his collection. But Arthur found himself cut off by a knock at the door followed by sounds of struggling as Violet Loo appeared wrestling through the opening with the double burden of two cups and saucers, catwalked across to the desk and set them awkwardly down. Coffee – and biscuits. She looked at Arthur in triumph. He thanked her and smiled but Da Cunha looked down with displeasure as if reading a bad omen in the murky contents of the cups.

He pouted. 'Ah yes. Perhaps henceforth Miss ... Miss ...?'

'Loooo,' Arthur offered helpfully. But saying it obliged him to purse his lips as though for a big, lingering kiss and he blushed furiously at the thought.

'... Miss Loo, instead of coffee, could we have Portuguese tea with honey and cinnamon. I think that ...'

Violet Loo turned on her heel huffily and stalked out. She was wearing shiny, red shoes today. You couldn't help noticing.

***

The boys came in a canoe far too big for them, exhausted and half incoherent from the journey. They were only about ten years old but the black girls had told them what to say. When Hare finally teased out what they meant, he rounded up half a dozen men and left at once. It was a hard paddle against the tide but a strong, following wind had sprung up and they buffeted through the choppy sea at a good pace with the roar of the surf like an angry beast away in the darkness. After half an hour, a flicker of flame appeared, far off and they headed towards it as a beacon, the waves now coming directly from the side and making progress difficult. Hare ordered them to put in and they beached the canoe and disembarked before setting off grimly on foot, pounding just above the waterline where the sand was firm, thinking to make better progress that way.

A bonfire blazed on the beach ahead, showering sparks up into the black sky, blotting out the swirling stars but showing longboats drawn up clear of the water. It lit up a scene from Breughel, with dancing, devilish figures silhouetted black against the raging flames. Other were sprawled on the sand, out of the firelight, drinking and fumbling in shadows. Screams and shouts, laughter and grunts merged with the steady farting of a brass band. As they drew closer, the Bacchanal revealed itself in its full horror. They were doing Scottish country dancing. Hare found something particularly hellish about a Scottish reel played on tuba and bugle and he broke into a run and burst into the ring of light like an Old Testament prophet returning down from the mountain and catching the Israelites with their golden calf, waving his pistol and screaming curses.

Going straight to the centre of things, he advanced upon the small boy enwreathed in the tuba and tore it from his terrified hands, flung it to the ground and turned to recognise Leisk coming towards him, with – of all things – an offered glass of rum and – unbelievably – a smile on his face. As the music tailed away and the band boys fled howling, he rushed at him and smashed it to the sand with his weapon.

'You swine!' He was shaking with rage. 'I'll teach you to mess with my women!' He waved his troops on with a broad sweep of the arm. 'Seize them, men!'

Nothing happened. He looked round and suddenly found that he was alone, a Wellington without grenadiers, outnumbered and the focus of enemy attention. His own men were deaf and blind to orders, busy fossicking in the shadows, anxiously trying to establish whether their own wives were part of this debauch as the women scattered and fled with faces covered, rustling off into the trees like startled rabbits and the men pursuing them. Hare froze in midstep.

Leisk laughed, knucklecracking and shaking off drops of rum from his fingers. 'Not so brave on your own are you?'

'I'm brave enough to take care of you.'

As Hare raised the pistol to fire, his lips twisted with hatred, right leg advanced in best duelling style, another figure stepped in from the side and swiped him smartly across the side of the head with a rifle butt and he went down, seeing stars, firing up into the real, now-invisible stars and, as he dived into unconsciousness, he thought he heard the black girls laughing. The sailors shouldered up the rest of the rum at their leisure and set off for home in their own boats, leaving Hare lying face-down in the sand. Some lit up cheroots and slapped each other on the back. It had been a grand night out with dancing, sex, drink and a good roughhouse to round it all off nicely. They would certainly be recommending Cocos to all their friends. After a while, the tuba-playing boy returned tearfully on tiptoe and stepped around the prostrate form to recover his bruised instrument and faded silently back into the trees, stroking it for comfort, while the stars sped on in their paths with cool indifference.

'Miss Loo. Tomorrow I shall be working at home. I wonder if you could come to the house in the afternoon about three o'clock so I can dictate some letters.'

It was a bold move. He had lain awake at night running it over and over in his head and rehearsed every part of it of course, everything said very matter-of-factly while looking down casually at his wristwatch, half-stifling a yawn, as if the most normal thing in the world. He watched her closely for any sign of deeper comprehension and caution on her part, any awareness that he was now one of the men her parents had warned her against. He had prepared all the necessary justifications, rationalisations, puzzlement at her reluctance, routes of withdrawal, just in case.

'I come your house?'

'Yes.'

'Tomorrow?'

'Yes.'

'For letter?'

'Yes.'

'Really, meh? Okay-lah. Can ready.'

***

'A rose has been stolen from my flower garden!' Hare stood on the flat roof of the house, threw up his still-bandaged head and howled to himself or perhaps the entire world. Arthur thought it was an odd way for Hare to put it, both sad and staggeringly lacking in self-knowledge at the same time.

After the party on the beach, Yani from Aceh had run off with one of Ross's men. She had not, of course, been stolen, she had begged to go. She remembered the black girls' words. Her new man was young and strong and passingly handsome and, that he would swiftly make her a mother, she did not doubt. All necessary competence had been fully demonstrated. When she dreamed of him she even loved his ears. The black girls had said that was the test and, as they knew the ways of the wider world, it seemed quite plausible to her that they were right.

Yani a rose? If so, then Arthur thought she was no wild rambler like Eileen, though she came not without thorns. Perhaps she was even the one who had tried to drown Hare that night in the lagoon. The black girls, after all, were from arid, landlocked country – water-fearing people who could not swim – whereas Yani was of hippy fisherfolk rootstock and wholly amphibious.

And was the harem really a garden where the beauteous, sunkissed heads of the girls were brought to flower just by constant, tender attention, preening, pruning and the eradication of pests? No, by now it was more a prison, a place of supervision and confinement. That rifle blow had addled something inside Hare's head. Gone were the days when the girls were free to wander like does in the forest and bathe in the limpid sea at will. Nowadays, they were restricted to the rocky beach within Hare's eyeshot. As a child, Arthur had sat through endless classes of religious instruction where God was the good and caring shepherd but they never explored the image to its logical conclusion to mention that a shepherd ends up fleecing and slaughtering his sheep and then devouring them and is often rumoured to abuse them in his boredom simply for perverse pleasure. And if Hare was to be seen as a loving horticulturalist, the fact should be recognised that, sooner or later, every rose gets manured and plucked.

Life on an island becomes very small. Hare's paradise atoll had now shrunk to the size of a maximum-security boarding house. Outside wars become domestic feuds. A misplaced word detonates lethal hatred. He had moved his family to Rice Island, minute, higher out of the water and had built – or rather his men had built – a defensive stockade made of sturdy driftwood and with a platform on the roof like a widow's walk. A fortress. But every fortress against the world is always a prison too for those who inhabit it. Up there, he had a cane chair and a telescope that unfolded with a series of purposive clicks as he scanned every dot on the horizon that might menace his peace of mind and announce trespassers on his tranquillity. He had ceased to mark the passage of the days and they now blended into a monotony of watchfulness. The girls, often sullenly penned up downstairs or in the yard behind the fence, came to hate that sound. Click, click, click. He sat there all day, mumbling to himself, sipping rum or brandy – never quite drunk, never quite sober. There was a constant, strange singing in his ears that he feared would drive him mad and he thumped his own head in vain to chase out the wailing sirens in his brain. A sighted canoe from the other settlement had him instantly on his feet, reaching shakily for his blunderbuss and God help any of Ross's men that ventured within range. The sail of a larger vessel prompted the ringing of a bell that summoned any women outside back inside the stockade, where he stood cursing and waving his arms, the gate barricaded until the ship had sailed again. The girls longed for the days when they had been driven out to gather coconuts in the hot sun. There was no peace for anyone any more, only long stretches of taut boredom. The domestic chronology of washday, cleaning day, salting day, pickling day had been destroyed. No longer was the house a place of girlish laughter. It was no way to live.

Hare could feel the tension building beneath him like a smouldering powder keg. He knew they were plotting and could not buy them off with a few trinkets as in the past. He had no way into their minds that were locked and sealed against him. He realised he was horribly alone, on an island within an island. There had been no supplies for months and rumours were rife of more major clearing houses going down, one after another, in both India and London. Traders, ever mobile, were defaulting on their debts and doing a runner. Even the Company wobbled but would be saved by its poor accounting as it was so large that no one could bring all the pieces of paper together at one time and in one place and prove it was effectively bankrupt. So it lumbered on like some great blind elephant from year to year. His brothers were heavily exposed in both London and Calcutta and his fortunes depended on theirs. The girls, with their different dietary demands, no longer prepared spicy dishes that were tear-jerking memories of their diverse homes. He knew they were only surviving because they collected shellfish and strange leaves and knew how to disguise them cunningly into various versions of the same dull meal.

Often, his guts went into spasms so that he had to run to the back and pump out pint after pint of searing fluid. They were still poisoning him, still getting it to him somehow. It must be the water. He must stop drinking water and double his vigilance. He would set mantraps around the house to stop people wandering about at night. But he would have to keep shifting them which would mean leaving the house unguarded while he did it in the dark. Could his own men be trusted? Ogilvie had claimed he knew nothing of the beach party but he was a practised liar. Hare had threatened to have the girls whipped but Ogilvie had said quietly that none of the Malay men would do it, he certainly would not and he should not force a confrontation on the issue or face rebellion from the male slaves. Some of the other workers, free and slave, had tried in the past to run away to Ross who always needed more labour but he had refused to take them in for fear of the consequences. But now that had changed since Yani. Hare decided he would gather up all the children and keep them in the stockade at night as pledges for their parents' obedience. He screamed for Ogilvie.

***

The doorbell rang.

Arthur started but determined to force himself to wait ten seconds before rising from his chair. Everything had been carefully planned. Bok had toddled off to his docks and ice cream treat, carrying a huge shopping bag. Arthur was thoroughly preened and carefully reruffled so as not to look too deliberate, nostrils and toenails reduced to civilised order. A rare and delightful breeze blew through the polished living room like a friendly ghost, assisted by the ceiling fan, ticking on its lowest setting unlike the one windmilling hysterically in Battersby's office. In the whispering hush, Arthur had needed a quick one to steady his nerves which meant he then had to desperately search through the whole house for a peppermint to hide the smell on his breath which made him hot and sweaty and more nervous all over again He sat and tried to read the newspaper. As usual there was no real news, just thick black headlines screaming of terrorist attacks brewing in the north again, all heavily sauced with plummy, dismissive comments parroted by Battersby and his like.

It rang again.

Violet Loo stood on the step, clutching her shopping bag. Her face was dewed with sweat from the walk. The imperfection reduced her ceramic untouchability. She looked slightly peeved that Arthur had answered the door himself as if that suggested she was not worthy of a proper servant's attention.

'Come in, Violet.' He froze. It had slipped out. He checked himself, smiling. 'I hope you don't mind my calling you that since we're not in a work environment. Let's be a little less formal.'

'Anything, lor.'

She was wearing high-heels that she kept on, treading dirt from the path over Bok's gleaming floor. They emphasised the stretched muscles of her golden calves. She must be wearing stockings despite the heat. He led her into the living room and pointed at a chair. She set down her bag and sat, primly, knees together as if at a church meeting. He would have to stalk her like a cat stalks a bird, moving so slowly as not to be perceived to be moving at all, doing nothing to startle her.

'Let me get you a drink.' The ceiling fan played with her hair, teasing it out of its perfect symmetry, making her even more flawed and so yet more desirable.

'Water only.'

He pushed through the door to the kitchen and went across to the fridge that sneered at him smugly, poured her a tall glass of refrigerated water, added sophisticated ice-cubes and took the opportunity to seize another quick slug of scotch from a bottle on the dresser. His trembling hands fumbled and dropped the cap that rolled away with a death rattle and hid. He left it, put the smirk back on his face and re-entered the living room, all calm assurance and iced water.

'Here you are, Violet.' He slid it tinklingly onto the table at her elbow. She touched it and mouthed distaste.

'Cold.'

'Yes it's nice and cold. I put ice in it for you, specially.'

'No. Is *cold*,' she snapped. 'Bad for you. You drink, get *angin duduk*. Can *diiie*.'

Angin duduk. It must be something like 'trapped wind'. 'Wind' in its various forms howled through the Asian mind and was held to be a terrible and constant menace to life in these parts.

'I see. Well, let it rest. It will soon warm up.'

It was curious the way every technological advance brought its own myths of retribution. His mother had believed with absolute conviction that the weather was ruined by radio waves pulsing through the ether, nowadays it was the testing of atom bombs. Science tried to impose a universal rationality on a disenchanted world but it was the unshackled variability of things that lay at the heart of the exotic and its charms, just as it was small imperfections that alone made Violet desirable. He picked up a file from the table and settled into the other chair.

'Let us chase up the drongo cuckoo business. I have the name of a birdwatcher on Cocos-Keeling who has worked with us in the past. Since we are being ignored by the management of the wireless station, perhaps we can get some sort of reply from him as a fellow enthusiast.' He smiled, luring her into a conspiracy of mutual interest.

Violet made a face again, stretched out one leg and admired it, looked bored. '*Sian*. What for you *tok kok*? What for you ask about stoopit bird again?'

Arthur gaped. 'What for? Well … It's because … What *for*?' Irritation sparked. Wait. This was the opportunity he had been waiting for to move on from work to more intimate subjects. He raised one eyebrow in a worldy-wise way and oleaginated low-voiced, 'If you don't want to write the letter, what would you rather do?'

She pouted like a child denied an ice cream. 'You don't ask me here for letter. I know what you want. I see way you look at me. Can.'

'Can? Can what?'

'Can! *Jialat!* Deaf is it?' She rose to her feet and, to Arthur's horror, briskly unbuttoned her blouse and shrugged it to Bok's impeccable floor in a stalking matador gesture. Her breasts peeked at him, pert, like two sweet children peering over a wall, wholesome not like – oh my God! – Salma. The remembered name acted like a bucket of iced water, dousing in *angin duduk* his rising enthusiasm that had been struggling to recover from its first shock. Violet kicked off her shoes and advanced, menacing, shoulder-swivelling, bra-loosening, a pouncing panther, a gurgle of hot blood in her throat. A dam had been breached and now he was to be swept away by a tsunami of foaming lust. Arthur leapt up and backed hastily away. My God! This was what it was to be Alexander Hare, attacked by his girls, an unwitting sex bomb with a long fuse. Was it possible she had established some mystical link to Anna and Maria?

'Don' *geh geh lah*. Men not much good but sometime woman need man. I never go with *ang mo* before.' She waved a hand dismissively, banishing his false modesty and seized him by the shirtfront, ripped. Buttons popped along with Arthur's eyes and rattled off the wainscoting like birdshot. This was not how he had imagined it at all. This was the nestling preying upon the cuckoo. He began to dodge around the dining table with Violet in relentless pursuit, a greyhound after a hare, as in an overacted amateur version of some G and S comic scene.

'But ... but ...'

A wheeze of laughter off to one side. They both span round in shock. It was ancient Bok, holding his shopping bag in one trembling hand, pointing at them with the other and shaking with laughter so that the curry leaves poking out did a little dance in sympathy. Theirs was the oldest story in the world but one he still found funny.

But wait. As she turned, open-mouthed, Violet's smoothly stockinged feet slipped on the immaculately polished floor. She pirouetted, lost her balance wobbled like a slowing top and, as her feet shot out from under her, went down with a bang that nearly – but not quite – covered her scream. Her head hit the side of the table, sending the drongo cuckoo papers flying and she lay, strangely pale, unmoving, with a pool of blood gathering like a halo round her temples. They stared down at her, both frozen in surprise and guilt. Arthur came to himself first.

'Help me, for God's sake, Bok.' They humped her over to the sofa, a hard rattan construction ill-suited to medical conscription, and stretched her out. Arthur was unsure whether to slap her face or not. 'Fetch some water.' Bok hobbled off. Arthur was suddenly aware of the untouched glass at his side, dipped a handkerchief into it and lay it softly across her forehead, as Bok returned with a bowl.

'It's alright, Bok. I've got ...'

He turned and saw that the old man was totally ignoring him and the prostrate woman and was down stiffly on his knees, tutting loudly, quacking outrage in Hokkien and wiping the mess off his treasured teak floor, fighting to save the waxed finish before the blood got into it and only pausing to glare at the trail of indentations Violet's high-heeled shoes had left in its surface.

***

As long as they were imprisoned by mere social convention and expectation, Hare's women accepted their fate, indeed were unaware that any such fate existed. As soon as these invisible barriers became real walls and locked doors and Hare's patrolling feet could be heard plodding over their heads day and night, constraint made flesh, the girls began plotting their escape. Freedom invaded their thoughts, became the counterpoint to Hare's constant steps, the stock material of their daytime conversation and the stuff of their night time dreams.

'It is,' said little Ayu, assuming the Africans' storytelling habit, 'like the tales of the Garuda bird. Garuda is huge and all-powerful. His wings cause the hurricane. He preys on mankind and gobbles them up without pity. Yet he can be slain by brave humans and rendered impotent by tiny mice who nibble away his wing feathers, so slowly that he does not notice, and they take away his power of flight. His sworn enemies are the serpents but by simply swallowing stones they make themselves so heavy that they are immune to his attacks.'

Anna was unimpressed. 'Uh? Mice? Stones? Why make things so complicated. We could just stab him in his throat while he sleeps and run away.'

'He has Ogilvie who is loyal to him and he would avenge him. Anyway, he almost never sends for one of us at night now. He has learned to watch out for concealed weapons and makes us even unbind our hair when we approach him. When there is moonlight, he sits on the roof and watches through his telescope. When it is dark, he sleeps with one eye open and listens for every sound.'

'We could start a fire to distract him and rush the gate.'

'There is no need to rush the gate. When there are no foreign ships, the gate is unlocked and we are sent out to gather coconuts. And where could we run to? That is his power over us. We have nowhere else to go.'

African Anna smiled. She knew what they were whispering about. The Bengkulu girl had come to her with such thoughts and she had sharpened and encouraged them.

On Sunday, according to the ancient dispensation, she and Maria went to divine service at the Ross house. Hare had sought to forbid it after the party on the beach but had been ignored and he dare not let himself be seen as one who would interfere with religion. The Muslims would not stand for it. Anyway, it was a way of finding out what Ross was up to. Naturally, the women invented freely as they returned and delivered their report.

'*Tuan* Ross has written to the Dutch, telling them you are selling arms to the rebels in Java and asking them to take over the islands and drive you away. He has written to the English, telling them *you* have been writing to the Dutch, inviting them in. He has sent word to your slaves that he will take them in if they run away and will pay them wages. He is trying to divide your house against itself.'

At the Ross settlement, the family and other Europeans sang weird psalms that made little sense, being full of language no one ever used and Mrs. Dymoke preached the discovery of evil in places where surely no evil could live. As usual, Maria and Leisk skirted each other with their share of forbidden knowledge and both girls concentrated their attention on Mrs. Dymoke over the teapot to which they were companionably invited. They did not know that two cups of different colour were kept for their exclusive use and ruthlessly scrubbed afterwards with lye soap.

'It is the children that are suffering, dear mother. He keeps them all locked up and they are wasting away. It breaks my heart. Many might be brought to God if only they were free.'

'But are they not born into the Muslim faith? John says we must never attempt to save their souls or they will have our heads in recompense.' She nodded like a self-approving child pleased to have learnt its lesson well and looked across to where her son-in-law sat with the men sipping disapproved-of brandy.

'Children are of no faith, mother. They are empty vessels that cry out to be filled with the truth. Look at us. We were born lost but now are found thanks to good people like yourselves. If only we could come and live with you in the true Christian way. And there are Hare's own children.'

The old woman gulped hot, sweet tea and coughed with a bitter face. 'Children? There are bastard children born of these ... these ... couplings? Spawn of the devil?'

Maria and Anna nodded in unison and made grave faces. 'Siti has ways of killing unwanted babies to make the blood carry them away but some of the girls hide their pregnancy until it is too late. To wash away the baby then would be to kill the woman. Have you not seen how fair some of the children are? The boys he makes into a brass band. You must have heard them playing. The girls ... well ... you can imagine. He hands them over to Siti, the mistress of his harem.' Inspiration struck, a memory of her days on the farm and she added, 'He calls it "ploughing them back in".'

'No!' The old woman closed her eyes, seeing it all in her mind, replaced her trembling cup in its saucer, lay it aside and breathed hard, gripping the table as if it were heaving in a sudden earthquake. 'Murder! Incest!' The words hissed with sizzling poison and she saw, in her mind, the smoking altars of Moloch scattered with spitted babies. 'But we have been sending back his runaways and it is only now that I have persuaded John to let them come over to us' A tremor of shock ran through the moustache of her top lip and she turned and called sharply to her son-in-law with a beckoning claw. 'John, come quick. Listen to this. I told you we must do something about Hare. We have already been punished by God with the storm for our inaction. There will be worse to come.'

Ross got up from where he had been sitting with the men, letting out a huge sigh of accumulated exasperation, and came across. 'What is it *now*, mother?'

***

'Shocking business, really,' said Macclehose. 'She's still in a coma and they don't know whether she'll pull through. I got a look at her hospital file. "Injuries consistent with the administration of a heavy blow to the head with a blunt instrument." The medical team say she'd obviously been interfered with. Of course, Grimsby and that servant of his will claim they took her blouse off for medical purposes but – I ask you – why do you need to expose someone's breasts in order to treat their head? Even the medically untrained who can't tell their scalp from their scapula would know that and Grimsby is supposed to have some sort of a medical background.' He leaned forward and dropped his voice. 'And, according to what my new chum Inspector Gan says, apparently, they'd tried to clean the place up in some clumsy attempt to get rid of the evidence. No, I'm afraid there's no way round it. There was monkey business afoot in that house. Not that I'm surprised. Grimsby was always a terrible womaniser. You didn't know? He hid it well, of course, the cunning bastard. Well I had it straight from his wife before she died, poor thing. What he put her through! She was a saint, that woman. But I didn't know he was violent too.' He shook his head in wonder at the ways of men less spotless than himself and took another pull at his drink.

Arthur had noticed a chill in the air despite the usual blistering heat of the season. When he walked into expat watering holes nowadays conversation died down as if someone had put a lid on a boiling pot. At the museum, Violet's absence from work and the reluctance of other staff to step into her shoes was the subject of muttered conversations around the building. Da Cunha was less circumspect.

'What's all this I hear about you suborning a subordinate, humping the help, Arthur? Or should I say thumping then humping the help? Or was it the other way round – was your humping before your thumping?' A man of the world, Da Cunha. He raised an eyebrow and put his feet up on the desk, playing with a pencil with gestures of judicious balance. Arthur was relegated by his own politeness to the usual folding chair in the corner. 'You can't expect to get away with racist stuff like that and hide behind your white skin these days you know. We natives have already peeked behind the curtain and seen the Wizard of Oz for what he is, a puny dwarf. You think you are a tolerant man, Dr. Grimsby, but the fact is that you merely treat everyone with equal contempt.

You are simply an equal opportunities bigot. At least the Japanese were not afraid to show how bad they really were.' He grinned and tapped his head as if suddenly conceiving a brilliant idea. 'Should I suspend you, do you think?' He looked through the window at the working gardeners. 'Do I have sufficient grounds?' He sucked on the pencil and blew out invisible smoke.

Arthur gnashed his teeth biblically. 'There was no humping, Mr Da Cunha, or thumping come to that, merely galumphing, an unfortunate accident caused by an excessively waxy floor. I should, anyway, have thought that any alleged sexual act across racial lines would be an unracist act by definition. I should also point out that you are not actually in charge of things as yet. Moreover, suspension could only be a matter for the board. Your role here is as an observer only and subject to confirmation on my retirement. I shall, of course, be writing a report on *you* before I leave.'

Da Cunha flashed an untroubled smirk with immaculate, ungnashed teeth. 'Hmm! Which will be ignored, I imagine, on the grounds of your own bad behaviour and incorrect attitude which I have noted and shall also report. But words are cheap, Mr. Grimsby, as the supply always greatly exceeds the demand. By the way, do I smell something on your breath? These things do not go unnoticed. Is that whisky or an unfortunate aftershave now you are beardless? You should switch to gin. It works well as aftershave too. People talk you know.' He tossed the pencil back onto the desk. It rolled onto the floor like a glove cast down as the challenge to a duel. They both sat and looked at it. He did not pick it up and neither did Arthur.

Alexander Hare junior hugged Siti with unfeigned warmth. The only acknowledged son of Alexander senior, she had known him since he was a baby, had indeed changed his breechclouts and dandled him on her knees back in Malacca in the days when her knees had been something to write home about. She had raised him as a Javanese child, not letting him crawl on the floor like an animal as white women did, and surrounding him with emblems of warrior manhood. Now in his twenties, he was a good-looking young man, golden-skinned, with his father's height and his mother's delicate features, good, frank eyes and an easy smile and the girls, herded together in the yard, were atwitter with excitement over his arrival. Perhaps there might be an opportunity for more Scottish country dancing, who knew? But to Siti, he was still her Mungil, her little one. He had come from Java aboard the *Borneo* with a mixed cargo and unmixed news. Before he had recognised the vessel, Hare had him in his sights and prepared to open fire with the swivel gun mounted on the roof. He was still up there, pacing up and down, suspecting some kind of a trap.

'I have letters for father from Uncle John. How is he?'

Her eyes darkened with concern. Her voice faltered and she clutched the East India Company badge around her neck like a sacred talisman. 'He is not himself, Mungil. You will be shocked to see him. He is thin and old and wild in his head.'

She turned in fear as heavy footsteps clattered down the stairs and a furious, bearded figure rushed into the room waving a pistol. 'Who is the master of that vessel? Is it one of the Rosses?

Don't my brothers know they are our sworn enemies? Are they mad to send him reinforcements?'

'Father! It is me, Alexander.' He stepped forward from the shadows into the patch of sunlight from the window and hugged him. 'Don't you recognise me?'

'Alexander? But *I'm* Alexander.' He pouted, nonplussed. Now someone was stealing his name. Tears started to flow down his cheeks. Then, somewhere behind the crazed eyes a memory snagged and bedded in like a barbed fishhook, slowing his bolting thoughts. He subsided onto a stool. 'Alexander? You mean Mungil?' His mouth gaped then smiled confusedly in recognition. 'What are you doing here? You are supposed to be in London or Java.'

'I brought the *Borneo* – and letters, urgent letters from your brothers.'

'What letters?'

Mungil reached into the leather bag slung around his neck and handed over a stack of correspondence tied up with string. They were yellow and travel-stained, some affected by damp. Many would be tedious duplicates, sent by different routes in the hope that one copy would get through and gathered up again along the way. Hare threw them onto the table in front of him with a snort.

'Later. I'll read them later. What news from "the great world"?' His mouth formed a bitter shape. 'Did you come via Malacca, that pot pouri of popery? What news of your mother? I'm sure she had much to say.'

'Never mind about mother.' The subject would only lead to

a pointless rant. Mungil was under firm orders from his uncles and gently insistent. '*Now* father.' He lay a calming hand on his father's shaking arm. 'You need to read them *now*. I will go and supervise the unloading of the cargo. We can talk later. The letters will explain everything better than I can.'

He shot Siti a worried glance, walked out into the sun and sighed wearily, made his way through the gate and climbed aboard the idling longboat. Ross was waiting to see him. That would not be an easy conversation either. The two houses that had always enjoyed such friendly relations were at daggers drawn. The Ross brothers and the Hare brothers had been, well, like brothers but few quarrels were as bitter as those within a family. Throughout the journey, as the men pulled on the oars and Ross's settlement drew closer, he wondered what attitude he should adopt. Belligerent? Conciliatory? His father's wild letters back to London could hardly be an accurate version of what had been going on and yet he felt the need to support him. But Uncle Ross was someone he had grown up to pay heed to.

The boat grounded on the sand. Mungil leapt into the water with an energy that he did not feel and made his way up to the house and tapped at the door in a perfunctory way. It was hard for him not to feel at home in John Ross's house. He stepped into the main room and, as his eyes adjusted, saw Ross at the table.

'Mungil! Come in lad! Come in and welcome. Did you have a smooth passage? All well with the ship?' They shook hands and sat and for ten minutes they chattered about nothing in particular as if just happening across each other in some London coffee-house. Then an awkward silence fell like a dropped anchor.

'It's father.'

Ross set his mouth in a thin line. 'I won't mince words. Your father's round the bloody bend, Mungil. Have you seen the stuff he writes in his diary?' He reached behind to a shelf and took down a sheaf of papers. They had known each other since he was just a little boy back in Malacca. Ross had bought him sweet cakes down by the port and later it was John Ross that taught him the rudiments of sailing.

'No, uncle. How would I ...?'

'It's the ravings of a madman.' He leant back and called into the kitchen for coffee and brandy. 'We have no cakes. My wife and mother-in-law hold them to be the diet of the Whore of Babylon. You remember? So no cakes any more.' He smiled and passed over the bundle of papers. 'Just look at it. It's in the scrawl of a lunatic. I don't have the latest entries yet, of course, which I am sure would be even more deranged, but he is convinced we are all conspiring against him, wishing his destruction and even spying on his every move.'

'But how ...?

'Oh well, I have a copy of it by someone in his household but that's by the way.'

Mungil blinked. Both these crazy old men were round the bend, driven over the edge by their festering, petty feud. 'Then surely the lunatic scrawl is not his but the copyist's and by implication the lunacy too. And if he believes himself to be spied upon, that merely reflects the fact that you ...'

Ross batted the objection away. 'Look. That, as I say, is by the way. He drives his whole household out of their reason with his wild behaviour. The point is that he's a danger to himself and to everyone else. He goes always armed with that loaded blunderbuss and sooner or later he will kill someone and then I won't answer for the consequences if it's one of my own people. Incidentally, his man Ogilvie hasn't been seen for a while and no one seems to know what has become of him. People say he walked into the sea. They had a big disputation just before he disappeared. Your father locks up his people but he's the one who should be chained up at night. They are getting restless again. You remember what happened at the Cape? It's happening again and it's only a matter of time before it bursts out again as it did there and who knows where it will stop,'

'Oh God!' Mungil had come with his bag stuffed with his own papers, bills for goods supplied to Ross, shipping charges for freight to Java. It would be a long, heated discussion. He could not face all that nitpicking, hairsplitting, hare-splitting …

The servant came, bringing a tray and waited politely, like an English butler, until the young gentleman had stopped tearing at his hair before she poured while Ross settled back in his chair and considered him. Perhaps it was rushing things but he would speak his mind anyway.

'Mungil, I have a proposal.'

'A proposal, uncle?' His hair was now as mad as his father's, emphasising the family resemblance.

'If you can secure that your father leaves the islands for good, taking him away with you and renouncing all further claims, I will buy his workers and his oil-pressing machinery at a fair price.'

'A fair price?'

Ross pursed his lips. 'The best price you will get from anyone on these islands, at any rate. You must appreciate you are selling the contents of a leaking vessel.'

'Hmm. And what of his women?'

Ross pouted. 'I have no interest in them except as workers or wives for the men. They may stay or go as they choose.' A glint came into his eye. 'Oh ... except for the two black girls. They are Christians and they must stay or I shall have no peace from my mother-in-law for the rest of my life.'

The two men grinned at each other. Mothers-in-law! Women! As men of the world, they understood these things.

'That is all very well but it is no use. Father will not go and I cannot make him.'

Ross grinned. 'Oh, I have a way to make him. Just leave that to me.'

***

Arthur was not unduly surprised to receive another summons to Battersby's office at the istana. Aida Binti Nasir, the beehived secretary, glared at him through her upswept glasses and reluctantly put down her knitting to consult her diary. Arthur wondered what you could possibly need to knit in this climate.

'Grimly, isn't it?

'If you like.'

She nodded in slow satisfaction and flared her nostrils. 'Ah yes, Mr. Battersby wants to have a word with *you*.'

She announced the glad tidings over the phone and carefully

watched with poised needles as he made for the inner office, as if fearful he might steal something along the way, plunging back into motion as he disappeared from view.

'Ah yes,' echoed Battersby and swivelled and sighed across the desk. 'Take a pew, Grimsby – er, Arthur.' He looked across at him with saddened eyes and kindly adjusted the desk fan so that Arthur received one end of the blast. With mainsail-sized ears like that, a fan must be a considerable danger to Battersby as he busybeed around the office. The atmosphere was familiar. It was like being detected in sin by the school chaplain who would not be angry, merely terribly, terribly disappointed. He half expected Battersby to launch into an account of the facts of life, hedged round with warnings of the perils to his body and soul of extra-marital sex.

'The repatriation people tell me you've chosen to ignore my advice and still not answered any of their letters,' he whined. 'What the hell's going on? Haven't I got enough to be getting on with? You will understand that no one wants odds and sods hanging around after their sell by date. Write to them for god's sake and get them off my back, there's a good chap.'

Arthur began to mouth excuses on pure reflex but found himself suddenly overwhelmed by an unfamiliar urge to brutal frankness. It was what he termed an 'Oh fuck it moment' when it just felt so good, so redeemingly human, to rip off the corsets of social expectation, let it all hang out and just tell the truth for once. 'If these are my declining years, Battersby, then I decline. Only those who expect something good from the world are in a hurry to correspond with it and I find that most letters these days can be ignored. I have learned, and let me share this wisdom with you, that almost all problems resolve themselves after a few days if you just ignore them. If it's anything urgent, people usually ring you up or write again. Perhaps *you* might learn from that, Battersby.' Of course, he had stopped answering the phone too but he hadn't been asked about the phone so he didn't mention that.

Battersby gasped, a bureaucrat who had spent his life building an unshakeable empire of paper from frenzied foolscap, a man for whom 'an administrative block' meant exactly that, was stunned by the outrageousness of the statement and shot him a look as though he were a priest who had bent over the host at the altar rail and sonorously farted. 'Well ... I ... That's as may be. Then there's this business of an attack – er – alleged attack on an employee. What's all that about?' He sucked worriedly on beaver teeth.

'She is a colleague, not an employee. And there was no attack. My man, Bok, who – as you know – is most reliable and *is* an employee, saw the whole thing and can confirm my version of events. Attack? Is that what she says?'

'That's just it. She doesn't say anything at the moment, Arthur. She's in a coma and that leaves other people's tongues free to wag. And I assure you they are wagging.'

'It's that damned Macclehose, isn't it? Going on about my "fancy birds" – a stupid misunderstanding, a joke of my wife's. As for the rest, that's hardly my fault is it? I should have thought your principal concern would be to stop any such slander and criminal libel against me by wagging not your own tongue but your finger.'

Battersby gaped and dithered. Arthur saw it was pointless and switched tack, undermined him with reasonableness as Eileen used to do in their endless, circular arguments. He smiled and spread his arms in gracious blessing. 'In fact, I am convinced that you are doing nothing to encourage these stories, old man, and should like you to know I am grateful for your continued loyal support. Be sure that I will make it known to everyone.' He rose to leave.

'Well. I ... That is to say ...'

Arthur relented. 'Look. All right. I'll write to the repatriation people, I'll go quietly but you have to do one last thing for me. Fix me a passage on the next Cable and Wireless supply ship from Singapore to Cocos-Keeling.'

Battersby frowned, suspicious. 'What the devil do you want to go there for? Ghastly hellhole. You should see the administration it still throws up even though, strictly speaking, it's officially not our pigeon but Australia's. More trouble and paperwork than it's worth to either of us.'

Arthur smiled. 'I have some unfinished business with one of my fancy birds that lives there.'

'I don't understand what you mean by "fancy birds"? Who are we talking about?'

Arthur shook his head and headed for the door. 'A real drongo cuckoo.'

'No need to be rude.'

On his way out, he stopped by the secretary's desk. Her gaze rose impassively from her knitting to his face but the fingers continued to flash away like – he though – those of Madame

Defarge as she greedily watched Marie Antionette mount the scaffold to her death. The thing she was producing grew before his eyes in hideous shades of yellow and blue like some timelapse film of a flatulent coral reef.

'May I ask ...? What are you knitting? Is it perhaps a wedding dress?'

She looked silent daggers or, at least, knitting needles.

'No? Then I hope it is a hat for Mr. Battersby. He can poke his ears through the holes on either side.'

'It's a tea-cosy,' she scowled.

But as he pushed through the door and out into the throbbing midday heat, he heard her laugh behind him, an unnerving sound and one far rarer than the haunting call of the drongo cuckoo on Cocos-Keeling.

***

Hare sat crumpled in a corner of the roof and stared out bleakly at the setting sun. There was a red, watery haze around it that made it look like a sore eye, an inflamed *mata hari*.

'All gone then? The London trading house, the Indian stock, the Dutch bank – everything?' He turned to his son in anger. 'How can it all be gone? Just a few years back, we supplied the whole force for the Company's invasion of Java. My brothers are cheating me, stealing from me. They think I'm a fool and you're in this plot with them. I should never have sent you to London. Your mother was right.' He never thought he would live to say that. 'It was a mistake.'

Mungil laid his hand over his father's. 'There was nothing to be done. Once the Indian trading houses started to collapse and default on their letters of credit, it was like a stack of dominos knocking each other down one after another.' A new domino theory. 'And the government did nothing, just talked of the change from a war to a peacetime economy and the inevitable stresses and strains on the markets. Then now there's the Dutch fighting in Sumatra, disrupting trade and doubling freight and insurance. There's nothing to be done by men of good will but pray for another major war in Europe to push up prices and restore normality.'

'There's no rush, I can carry on here. We can keep going on the sale of coconut oil alone. They need it for the Javanese lighthouses.' His eyes widened, seeing it all. 'I can make the children work too instead of sitting around idle in the brass band. And the slaves don't need to pray on Fridays, they can get off their knees and go out and work instead. With more machinery we can increase output. The possibilities are endless.'

Mungil shook his head and held down his father's fluttering hands. 'Father, father. It's over. The ships have gone, sold off to pay our debts. This is the last voyage of the *Borneo*. We can no longer keep you supplied or ship out the oil. Anyway, they have coconut oil of their own enough in Java or, better, whale oil. Coals to Newcastle and whale oil is the future. You must leave this place and come away with me.' He brightened. 'But Uncle John says that when God closes a door, he opens a window. I will look after you. I trade under my own name in Batavia. There is still money to be made.'

'Leave?' He looked around wildly. 'Leave? Never!'

Gently. 'It's the only way.'

'But what of my family?'

'*We* are your family.'

'I mean my girls and the other slaves. I cannot sell them. It would break their hearts to leave me.'

Mungil blinked. He hardly thought so. How could father believe that when they were running away at every opportunity – men and women? 'You know full well they are not your slaves any more. You signed those documents in Bengkulu and the Cape confirming they were free labourers, otherwise they would not have let you bring them in. You know that full well.'

'Ah!' A cunning glint lit up his eyes. 'But *they* don't.'

'Oh father! The world has changed. You cannot stay here. You cannot take them to Java. The Dutch still hate you. The Company still hates you. No British colony will let you in with slaves, nowadays, since the Maritime Act. *They* can either stay or go according to their choice but *you* must go with me. Look at yourself. You are not happy here.'

Hare gulped brandy and grasped his son's arm. 'There are the Spanish colonies. They are still places where they cherish human liberty so a man is free to have as many slaves as he wants there. South America!' A sudden, wild idea gripped him. 'Do they have coconuts in South America? I know a little Portuguese. They must have lighthouses. If not, I know how to build lighthouses.' His face lit up with the brightness of a thousand lighthouses all ablaze with his coconut oil.

'It is too late, father. The moment has passed.' Mungil

smoothed his father's wild hair, patting it down. 'This is all fantasy, crazy daydreaming. Mother is waiting for you in Malacca. She has always been waiting.'

Hare threw himself back in his chair and fat tears wobbled down his hollow cheeks. 'Your mother? Let her get the better of me? No. I would rather die.' He sat up like a dog that smells a rabbit. 'The Carolinas! They still have slaves there! We could go to the Carolinas, they even speak English of a sort there, don't they?'

Mungil quietly picked up the blunderbuss leant against the table, as if by accident and laid its snout carefully across his knees. 'Father. It's over. It's all over. It's time to go *home*.'

***

Bok was uncomfortable, running his finger round the collar of his shirt and grinning with sparse teeth. He was used to sitting across the big table from *Tuan* Grimsby on Saturday mornings when they went through the household accounts for the week and sorted out the expenditure recorded in Bok's little book. But this was not a Saturday morning but a Friday night and it was unclear what this was all about. It seemed unlikely there would be the usual ticking of the price of onions and discussion of the bargains to be had in tinned cheddar. All departure from strict routine was a source of anxiety and Bok strained to understand the *tuan's* difficult English through the sailcloth of his failing hearing.

'It's time to go home,' Arthur said, and took a suck at his glass of whisky like a weasel sucking at a rabbit's brain. *Tuan* was drinking a lot these days as was documented in the stack of empty bottles beside the gas stove, too valuable and useful to throw away even if their precise usefulness remained to be defined. Anyway, *tuan* found it hard to throw anything away so there was also that neat pyramid of Oxford marmalade jars ready to be moved to the space under the house tomorrow.

Home? Bok nodded. He *was* home and not moving. The Japanese war had not moved him.

'We are all leaving. I have had a letter – an official letter from government. I don't know exactly when but soon. This house goes back to the government and we both have to leave. It is in the letter.'

Bok had heard talk of such things for years. Politics did not bother him. He was a man of everyday concerns – the price of things in the market, the drains, the eternal battle against the moths in *tuan's* closet. They were being troublesome again and he must get some fragrant leaves to keep them away.

'I stay.'

Arthur shook his head tiredly and swigged further patience. 'Noo. You cannot stay. You work for me, not the government. They say we must both go – probably by the end of July.'

'I stay. If I no work for government, government cannot tell me to go.'

'Nooo. You must go too. The house belongs to government. But before that, there will be much work to do, packing things up. Too many things.' He looked round in despair at his own hopeless 'fiddlefaddle'. The books would be the main problem. He did not even know where he would be going. England? There was nothing for him there but a cold, uncongenial past, no warm resonances of coming home. Unlike Hare, he belonged to a proper English family whose members detested each other and reunited only to resharpen their feuds on festive occasions. And shipping liverspotted English books from the tropics to England, their pages curled with damp? An absurdity. Coals to Newcastle. Who had said that? Coals? He wanted to burn the lot after years of writing them and just fling a blazing torch back through the door as he walked away, a suitable funeral pyre but perhaps with too many Nazi overtones. 'We will need to bring in someone to help then ship them off to the Chinese College perhaps. It is too much for two old men like us.'

Bok bristled. 'No need help. I stay. Like before with Japanese *tuan*. You go. I stay.'

Arthur let his shoulders sag and a terrible weariness crept into his voice. 'No. Please try to understand. Please just listen. They will not let you stay. I know you are attached to the house. I am too. But time's winged chariot – I mean times are changing, Bok, and we have to make way for … whatever.' Not much of a summary of the tangled swirl of current events, really. 'Do you have family?' Arthur felt a twinge of shame that he had no idea about Bok's past life or human relationships but surely all Chinese were obsessed with family? This scene must be being repeated all over the land as what the communists called 'the bloodsucking leeches' finally drew in their fangs. 'Children? Brothers? Sisters?'

'Nephew got.'

'Well there you are then.' He smiled and slapped both hands flat on the table, the problem solved. 'A fine, young nephew you say? Perhaps you could go and live with him? Is he in Singapore? That would be nice, wouldn't it? Perhaps he has children. They would keep you young. You could keep an eye on the house too.'

'Far. Over causeway. In north.' Bok threw his hand up as if pointing to a distant star, so distant as yet to receive a name.

'Even nicer! They say it's quite lovely up there, away from all the noise and dirt of the city.' Apart from the gunfire and the bombs of the terrorists, of course, and the beatings and beheadings rumoured to be handed out by frightened British troops, their pink knees knocking in their shorts. He drained his glass and refilled. Even to his own ears, his voice was getting slurred. 'I shall naturally make a generous settlement to help you out. My own plans are a little vague at the moment, Bok, but I feel sure my future has to be one without the luxury of servants. New times. Different times. But we must look after each other, the two of us, as best we can.' He reached across, swaying awkwardly, and placed his hand on Bok's thin shoulder. 'Please, think about it. Think about what we can both do for the best.'

'I stay.'

***

'We are only slaves according to the law of the Dutch. This is not Dutchland – Holland – so no one is a slave here.' Maria waited for Ayu to finish translating and stared out at Hare's workmen who looked doubtfully back at her in the flickering torchlight. She was a woman. She was black like a devil. In this light she was just eyes and teeth. What did she know of such things, men's things?

Some squatted. Others stood and held machetes and hoes slung over their lean but muscular shoulders. Elephants in chains. One chewed betelnut and spat languorously. It was not clear whether this was a comment on what had been said. A man with one eye and a deep scar across his cheek, screwed up his face. 'Java is not Holland either but we were slaves in Java too.'

'And this is not Java either. There are no Dutchmen here. Here, the only laws are the laws you want to make for yourselves. Here there is no one to oppress you with violence.'

She shot an acknowledging smile at Ayu. 'We are like the mice that silently ate the feathers of the Garuda bird. We have already taken away its power, Hare's power, to hurt you. The Ross's say they will accept you on good terms. All you have to do is drive Hare away. He is weak. His sailors will not support him and you do not need to fear them or the cannon of the ship. His son who commands it has sold him to the Rosses. So who is the slave now?'

They murmured to each other. The one-eyed man called out, 'You are witches. We all know you are witches. Why should we trust you?'

In the dramatic shadows of torchlight, everyone was a witch. 'I thought men with one eye were witches?' Laughter. 'So I have been told. Or barren women. Or old widows. If you had trusted us at the Cape would you be here at all now and in this bad situation?' A grudging grumble of assent. 'No. But you did not listen and you went back to your master with your tails between your legs so he treated you like dogs. And if we were witches would you not wish us to be on your side rather than against you? So let me tell you about your children and what happens to children in that house.'

***

The old man down by the docks had not told Bok how many of the American sleeping pills he should use, so he poured the whole bottleful into the *tuan's* whisky and shook it up. At first nothing happened. They just lay there and slept, sullenly incriminating. Bok began to panic. He would have to pour it away and pretend he had dropped the bottle by accident and *tuan* would be angry. Then, grudgingly, they began to fall apart and dissolve, leaving only a slight cloudiness that lingered no matter how much further shaking was used. He unscrewed the top and sniffed at the mixture experimentally but could detect nothing but the fiery spirit. The pill bottle was small and the whisky bottle was large but only a third full. *Tuan* would easily get through that in the course of an evening and so feel the benefit of the whole dose. Anyway, better too much than too little.

It was wrong of the *tuan* to try to send him away after so many years, a form of unfaithfulness, a betrayal of trust to one who had always kept faith. He could not live with his nephew, anyway. Chin Peng as the *tuans* called him – sort of 'Joe Bloggs' as the English troops said – but really Ong Boon Hua, would be in the jungle with his guerrilla soldiers and Bok was a city boy, a Singapore boy. What would he do in the jungle where floors were made of dirt, polish grenades and clean rifles and run away from tigers? Moreover, he had to look after the house. Its bones were his bones, old and brittle perhaps, but still they held firm and they had grown into each other through long, slow years of living together and sleeping side by side like an old married couple. Of course, it had not worked out that way with *tuan* and *mem*.

He went back to his room and carefully copied out the names of the ships he had collected in the harbour today and put the paper in his shirt pocket so he would not forget to take the list to the toddy shop tomorrow and give it to the owner who would send it on to little Boon Hua out in the jungle.

Of course, Boon Hua was not so little now – really quite an important man too – and occasionally his picture would appear in the paper, upping the price on his head or announcing new talks with the government, or declaring peace or declaring war again, but, unlike politics, family was family and could be relied on and Boon Hua had never forgotten uncle Bok who used to buy him ice-creams when he came to the city as a baby. When *mem* had tried to make *tuan* fire him, he had sent a letter to Boon Hua, telling of her journey to the north. There had been a tree across the road, blocking it off, another toppling behind to cut off retreat and men in green uniforms had ambushed her car on a long stretch through the jungle and briskly shot all the occupants before melting away into the friendly, matching undergrowth. The government was surprised. That area was supposed to have been long 'pacified' and free of 'bandits'. He wondered whether they had explained to her why she was being shot – but no, they, themselves, would not have been told and then she would not have been kept in suspense for very long. He had given the house a special polishing to mark the news. Without her, it had heaved a great sigh of relief, whispered thanks in his ear in the creaking of beams and swiftly resumed its quiet and calm progress through time – you could hear the steady tick of the big, antique, English clock again as it echoed through the empty bachelor rooms. It was the beating heart of the house and his job was to ritually wind it once a week on Sunday night with the big brass key of which he was guardian, to bring the last week to a close and open the door on another. The kitchen was now entirely his again. Without the *mem*, there was no need for him to wear those stupid hot clothes she had insisted on, just in case she pushed her nose into the kitchen and found him in the comfort of his underwear. But, since *tuan* had started drinking, he would often spill whisky on his floor which was very bad for the polish and could not be tolerated. And now there was this business with the new woman and talk of him being sent away. There could be no doubt this was the woman's doing. Certainly, a man needed a woman – he himself had one once a year – but anyone could see this one was trouble and disturbance.

So now it was time for *tuan* to go too before he could send him away and it was only fitting that the whisky should do that job. He went across to the thin, hard bed. When the time came, this was the bed he would die in and that time would be soon. There was comfort in knowing which bed you would die in. He slid between the smooth sheets, closed his eyes and went immediately to sleep with his hands folded on his chest and, on his face, the still, small smile of a child that dreamt of ice cream.

***

They came at night, out of the darkness, and with faces blacker than the night itself, and led by a terrifying man with one eye and a machete. Thunder crackled in the distance and lightning hissed down into the sea. Dogs barked a warning but dogs here were ignored, always bad-tempered as made to subsist on a diet of fish. There was no shortage of tree trunks on Cocos-Keeling and they rushed from the beach and used one to break down the gate of the stockade with a single thudding blow. The act somehow lightened the mood, made it all into a sort of team game at a village fête and they gave a great cheer as it joyfully splintered and flew open. The children swarmed out like mice released from a trap to be grabbed up and hugged. Arthur understood witnesses described the early days of the French Revolution in similar terms.

Alexander Hare was hustled away by his son under protest from the sally port on the other side and transferred to a longboat in the spattering rain, his dignity further compromised by stumbling over the hem of the overlong, new nightshirt his son had brought him. It is unclear whether the fire was started deliberately or by some act of carelessness but the dry wood and bamboo of the house blazed swiftly and collapsed into a great pyre that then exploded to the four winds as the flames reached the powder store. Hare's island sultanate left no traces.

The next day would bring negotiation over the smoking embers and the choice of a passage to Java or a covenant with Ross but by then Hare was sitting out in the lagoon, sidelined, racked with fever and asking himself why paradise had borne such bitter fruit as he chewed on his sense of the ingratitude of women. Small wonder, then, that his ensured rage had been drawn into his gums and given him a terrible, unsugared toothache.

***

Arthur puzzled over how Hare's people had reacted to the end of the settlement. The black girls, certainly, would have rejoiced, having finally achieved their aim of bringing the House of Hare to its knees and finding – as they thought – a way off the islands. Perhaps there had been wild celebration in other quarters too but more probably just confusion since no one knew quite where they stood. Siti, of course, had remained loyal to Hare and left with him as did a Cocos daughter, Fatima, who would end her days in London. The slaves were still unaware that they were documented as legally free and had, indeed, just burned all the lavishly signed and sealed evidence that might have proved it. Ross felt no need to tell them, nor would he for years to come. Normally provenance from a fine collection adds value and Hare's ladies should have provided a rare windfall of available wives for the many unwed men of the islands – though as compromised women they might well have been scorned – but what would become of them if they returned to Java aboard the *Borneo*? Seen from afar that had been a rosy prospect but from close up perhaps less so. Would they be truly free or risk being snatched back into slavery the minute they set foot ashore, being seen merely as someone else's lost property, money carelessly dropped in the street? If truly free, how would they survive in a hard world? What had they left to sell? Would they come to dream regretfully of the security and ease that came from being the official concubine of a rich man? Would they even have believed that Java was the true destination of that ship they were now urged to board? They had been tricked before when coaxed aboard for the voyage from the Cape. There were stringent laws against bringing adult, male slaves into Batavia – on security not humanitarian grounds – but the children would be fair game to end up in the slave market there, torn from the arms of their parents and sold on at a good price – especially any of Hare's own fair-skinned progeny. Their brass band skills would be an added. incentive since everyone loved a slave with trained lips.

No wonder, then, that many of the more realist elected to stay on Cocos and throw their lot in with Ross and his colony of New Selma, named after the mythical ancient settlement of the Shetlands, rather than Batavia, named after the mythical ancient settlement of the Dutch. There had even been a formal ceremony of a sort, brass band playing to Mrs. Dymoke's tight-lipped disapproval, swearing of oaths, based on God's covenant with the Israelites of old, whereby Ross had appointed himself their master for all time to come. 'Thou shalt have no other employer before me.' As Moslems, most would not have recognised the parallel or seen what was the reinstitution of a very Dutch monopoly.

Arthur set down his pen, damp with sweat, and replaced it with a glass of iced scotch that also sat and sweated with streaming condensation. The fridge in the kitchen thudded and strained against the heat as if against terminal constipation and its vibrations set the glass irritatingly atremble. In France, it was said, offenders might legally claim the arrival of the hot *mistral* wind as mitigation for their crimes of passion. In Singapore, they should extend the same status to the absence of any wind. Even the gasping fan offered no relief for the air itself was heavy and soaked with humidity – you could wring it out like a hot, wet flannel. It was one of those nights when you fantasised about just sitting in a tub of iced water, when the mind refused to make the leap denied by the senses to believe you could ever have felt too cold anywhere on this earth. He rose, panting, and took both glass and bottle into the bathroom and ran a bath, the tap coughing and spluttering against the taste of the bitter rust from the old tank. He put his hand under the splashing water, tried hard to coax forth the image of an iced mountain stream and swept it over his face that felt rough and unkempt. The beard was growing back and he realised he had not shaved for days. No one was looking at him. The water was determinedly tepid no matter how long it ran. He took off his clothes, damp with sweat, dropped them on the floor and climbed into the tub, his body all ugly angles.

The African girls, Maria and Anna, would have been most put out, of course, when the terms and conditions of the covenant became clear. Having used their baptism as a weapon against Hare and a way of driving the Ross's into active opposition, they were now hoist on their own petard, denied escape from the islands they so hated and incorporated into the godswept and joyless household regime imposed by Mrs. Dymoke. Arthur imagined them, cursing Hare afresh as he sailed away, raging against their new domestic servitude but brought to their own knees in prayer three times a day and assailed by constant warnings against the bleak universality of sin, the fury of God and the provocation that lay in taking pleasure in life. Perhaps they found ways of dividing the house of Ross against itself with infinite slowness, tortoises not hares, as they had the House of Hare itself. Perhaps they enjoyed consoling encounters of rough and mindless physicality with passing sailors or even the Javanese men who would not actually marry them because of their terrifying black skins. Arthur hoped so.

He settled back in the water and poured more scotch, glowering at the joke plastic duck that Eileen had bought him, nesting smugly by the taps. With its cartoon, generic plumage it had always annoyed him and seemed to sneer at the very idea of serious ornithology. Perhaps that was Eileen's intention.

Hare had been carried away on the *Borneo*, babbling feebly of his violated rights and with Siti at his side but had escaped domestic incarceration in Malacca and achieved some sort of tolerated existence in now-Dutch Bengkulu, the colonial powers having swopped their colonies – Bengkulu for Malacca – like little boys their marbles. But perhaps there would have been enough reminders there of the days of wealth and Raffles and English rule to comfort him, monarch of all he survived, in the tight, little settlement perched on the coast. Siti would have stayed – her need being to have someone to look after. He was said to have died shortly afterwards during his wanderings in the Sumatran jungle. Was it from a wild beast or a fever? No one ever knew. And what was he doing in the jungle anyway? Was he chasing after more exotic women or perhaps he had taken up birdwatching? No corpse had ever been found, the story being that he had simply been rapidly interred among the trees, as circumstances required, in an unmarked grave, now lost. Was it perhaps revenge exacted by the relatives of young Ayu after she found her way back there and told her tale of Cocos-Keeling and they crossed krises with her oppressor? Arthur toyed with the fanciful idea that he might even have been kidnapped and carried off to end his days as a slave of Ayu's people in expiation of his former crimes, the world turned on its head. Would that have brought self-knowledge and guilt or would it just have confirmed his conviction that the world was unfair towards him? He chuckled at the conceit and soaped his thin arms and was suddenly aware of his own heartbeat echoing off the sides of the white ceramic tub like some great, muffled kettledrum throbbing inside a cave. The scotch was making him skittish but sleepy. He no longer slept at night. He reached out and drained the bottle.

There was a big lake in Bengkulu that some called the *Danau Dendam Tak Sudah*, 'the lake of unending revenge', so named as housing the vengeful spirits of two wronged teenage lovers driven to kill themselves there for a bottomless passion the hostile world would not suffer to be. Love was such an almighty pain in the arse, a disease that often proved fatal, whereas its delights were transitory and no match for the abrasions of life or perhaps it was more like a Buster Keaton film with flying sperm replacing flung custard pies.

Of course, others claimed the name of the lake simply came from *Dam Tak Sudah*, 'the dam that remains unfinished', because the dilatory Dutch administration had never got round to completing the project, the money draining away into some gin-soaked official's pockets as into a swamp. That left the fertile minds of the locals free to embroider the bare facts into some nice, historical sampler for the young to sigh over and promote a cheesy, puppy-eyed tourist trade of misunderstood young love. Arthur chuckled again. He remembered the lake as cool and flower-filled, with floating lilies and dancing dragonflies, a bit like the ponds of Hampstead in high summer. He had swum in it once on a field trip after a long, hot day on the road and now kicked his legs against the bathwater in remembrance, then lay back and let it gush over his head, taking him back to Bengkulu where Hare had breathed his last, back perhaps to the ultimate safety and comfort of the womb. As he sank under, he felt the lake finally fill him with peaceful relief. He embraced it, inhaled it, drifted sweetly away.

It was some time after midnight that Bok rose from a strangely troubled dream and came through the bathroom door. The bare lightbulb was still blazing and buzzing pitilessly overhead. *Tuan* lay encased in a lozenge of clear water like one of those strange aspic dishes he sometimes brought home from Cold Storage, frightening, soft paperweights that slithered and squirmed to the touch like a boiled seaslug. He resisted the urge to pick up the shed clothes from the floor but could not help using the discarded shirt to mop up a spill of water on the floor before dropping it back. He surveyed the scene carefully and thought briefly before taking away the bottle at the end of the bath and replacing it with an old, empty one from the kitchen, one without traces of sleeping pills. *Tuan* would have just swallowed the pills whole, not dissolved them first. He turned off the light and closed the door. No wait. That would not do. He returned and switched the light back on again, flicked the possibly incriminating glass into the water, shut the door, stood on the ladder from the kitchen, reached through the transom with a broom handle and pushed the bolt home from the inside before letting the transom swing shut and snap to. In the morning, when the Malay gardener came, he would call him into the house and make him break down the door and discover poor *tuan*. That would damage the bathroom door which troubled him but it could be promptly and easily mended as identical door-fastenings were cheaply on sale in the market. He would buy one tomorrow. He went back to his room and slid smoothly back into his bed like a well-greased bolt.

***

'There will have to be an inquest of sorts, naturally. There's no getting round it.' Battersby regarded the whole matter of Arthur's death as an act of personal spite. 'As if we didn't have enough to deal with and at a sensitive time such as this, too. Frankly, we could all do without this, Inspector Gan. You're a smart young fellow, straight from Hendon training college I believe, best police college in the world. Show me what they taught you up there. What do you think?' It was time to encourage the new guard, bring them on, build them up with a bit of responsibility.

The eager, young, Chinese police inspector leaned forward. He crackled with freshness as if come brand new from the inspector factory in a clean, sealed, cardboard box wrapped in crisp tissue paper. His uniform was immaculate, the tags gleaming, hair neatly Brycreemed to attention. 'I have written an outline of the case for you, sir. I think it can be quickly disposed of.' He offered a trim file, clamped top and bottom between perfectly manicured hands, resisting the attempts of the fans to scatter its contents.

Battersby rolled his eyes behind half-moon glasses and waved it away. 'No time for that, I'm afraid. Too much on my plate as it is. Just give me the gist of your investigation and the conclusions.' He smiled to himself. In the old days, he would have made a damning warning note in Gan's file for the next Brit, 'Too clever by half' or some such to allow them to damp down the ambition. Nowadays, you weren't allowed to do that. Those files would be left behind when the Brits went home and one shouldn't be openly rude.

The inspector looked disappointed to see his homework refused but sat up straight and concentrated hard. 'According to Dr. Macclehose's report, actual cause of death seems to be drowning, though Dr. Grimsby had previously ingested a substantial amount of scotch, mixed with barbiturates in what would have almost certainly proved a lethal dose had he not fallen under the water.'

Battersby raised a disapproving eyebrow and sucked air over his teeth. 'Are you suggesting suicide? Don't like the sound of that, Gan. A messy suicide is the last thing we need at a time of happy transition such as this. Suicides make everyone a lot of unnecessary work – all those loose ends. It always puzzles me how people can be so selfish.'

The inspector resumed swiftly. 'Arguing *against* a suicide, is the absence of any kind of note. It seems that the deceased had been working at a piece of historical research just before his death. Indeed, it was left unfinished on his worktable by the demise.'

Battersby nodded. 'Good point. Arthur was a chap who loved

the sound of his own manuscripts and once he started something, he always saw it through to the bitter end. He wouldn't miss a chance like that to spout off with some great, rolling memorandum of his numerous griefs. I suppose we should be grateful really. Anything in the stuff he was writing to shed light on his mental state?'

'Well, a lot of it seems to be about women.'

'Women, you say? Hmm. Well, bundle it up and ship it off to Da Cunha at the museum where no one will ever see it again. He seems to be a sound chap and doing a grand job over there.'

'If I may, sir, there are two odd points – small points but the sort a policeman notices. The first is that he put the top back tightly on the empty scotch bottle after he finished it. He would have felt very drunk and uncoordinated by that stage. It seems a strange thing to do.'

'Not in the least. Force of habit. A mere reflex.' He threw his reading glasses down on the desk and rubbed his eyes to show what one of those looked like.

'The other is that no bottle for the pills was found though the house was thoroughly searched. You would have expected to find it in the bathroom.'

Battersby yawned. 'Were the pills prescribed by his doctor?'

'No, sir, though people said he had complained of sleeping badly.'

'There you are, then. Small, backstreet chemists often just dole out a few pills in a twist of paper. God knows, you can buy anything in Singapore if you know where to go. We've tried to stop it. Can't be done. Like as not, he just flushed the paper down the loo after he took the pills. Another reflex.' He resumed the glasses and beamed through them at what was still an orderly world.

'There is also the matter of Dr. Macclehose's report. According to the post-mortem, signs of extensive and progressive damage to both temporal lobes were found, indicating a possibility of Küver-Bucy syndrome.'

'What the hell is that?' It was odd the way the locals sometimes astonished you with the unpredictable shallows and depths of their vocabularies. He had gone to the chemist's once and asked for something for heartburn and the Indian pharmacist had advised him to go immediately to the hospital and see a cardiologist. So he knew 'cardiologist' but not 'heartburn'. Odd.

'Apparently, it's a mental condition characterised by confusion, dizziness, extreme passivity and ... er ...' Inspector Gan looked around wildly.

'You mean he went mad, doolally. I wish I had time to go mad. Come on man. Out with it, quickly. We haven't got all day. What else?'

Beads of sweat dotted the policeman's unlined forehead. 'Well, sir, a diagnostic feature of the syndrome is frequently that the afflicted are driven to make totally inappropriate sexual advances – indiscriminately and to both sexes.' The young Chinese blushed and looked down hard at his knees.

'What? Arthur Grimsby? Stuff and nonsense. The least sexual man I ever met.'

The inspector cleared his throat and asserted himself reluctantly. 'Permit me to observe, sir, that the accused – I mean the deceased – was recently involved in a case of possible sexual assault against a fellow worker. Moreover, I have checked the museum records and the last official purchase made by Dr. Grimsby was of a cloth acquired from someone known to us as a notorious transvestite prostitute from Bugis Street. I have made extensive enquiries – we keep a suitably sharp watch on that location as you can imagine – and established that Dr. Grimsby had been seen repeatedly in that area of late.'

Battersby gaped. 'Arthur? Good god! He was using museum money to pay for prostitutes!' He paused and chewed on air. 'Hmm, I think there's no need to drag all this out in public, causing distress to the family and so on and blackening the otherwise good name of an honourable public servant. A man should at least be discreet where he cannot be moral.' He clasped his hands together and leaned forward to deliver his verdict. 'What I see here, inspector – and do correct me if I'm wrong ...' He paused to indicate that this was not a serious possibility, '... is the tragic case of a man suffering from a brain tumour that resulted in confusion leading to an accidental overdose and drowning. I'll have a word with Macclehose and ask him to sharpen up his report in that direction.' He leaned back and smiled loftily. 'Well done, young man. You are the future, young Gan, and tidying all this away efficiently could do your career a lot of good, you know.'

Inspector Gan gave a dazzling schoolboy smile of gratitude. 'Thank you, sir.'

'Who found the body?'

The inspector looked down at his notes. 'His manservant, sir, a Bok Ong.'

'How strange! Arthur and I were talking about him only the other day. Been with him for donkey's years apparently, frightfully loyal. Salt of the earth. This will be a bit of a blow to him, I expect. It's long before your time, of course, but he was terribly brave under the Japanese and did all sorts of good work at great personal risk. I suggest you have a quiet word with him, just gently jog his memory a little and remind him of how his master was looking forward to a happy retirement back home and had all sorts of wonderful plans for the future, so he can tell us all about it at the inquest. I'm sure he'll want to save Arthur's good name from embarrassment. And I tell you what, I think I can probably manage that gong the man should have got years ago. I'll slip it in before the Independence avalanche of awards. A fine example of Her Majesty's Loyal Chinese.'

Gan looked puzzled. Why should a manservant want to be given a musical instrument? There was no denying that sometimes the British were extremely odd.

Battersby rose behind his desk, indicating the interview was over. Gan came to attention and executed a smart salute at which Battersby squeezed out a deprecating, beaver smile.

'Ah, no, young man. I am a purely civilian administrator and we are speaking purely informally. A handshake is good enough for me, man-to-man.' They gripped mutually and the inspector's eye was caught by an extraordinary object on the top of the desk, a thing of lurid colours, knitted in wool. Battersby followed his gaze down.

'Ah yes. Apparently, it's a hat. My secretary knitted it for me.' His voice dropped to a confidential, man-to-man whisper to match the handshake and a condescending smirk passed between them. 'Frightfully kind of her of course but what *can* the woman have been thinking?'

Also by Nigel Barley

Toraja: Misadventures
of an anthropologist
in Sulawesi, Indonesia

In the Footsteps of
Stamford Raffles

Snow over Surabaya

Island of Demons

The Devil's Garden:
Love and war in
Singapore under the
Japanese flag

Rogue Raider: The
Singapore Mutiny and
the audacious Battle
of Penang